Dear Reader,

All my books are a labor of love, but this one qualifies more than most. I adore a white Christmas, a guitar-playing cowboy and a holiday-themed wedding. I've crammed all that, and more, into this story!

If there's anything better than a rugged cowhand, it's a rugged cowhand with a guitar braced across his denim-clad knees. Combine the body of a god with the soul of a poet and you have Trey Wheeler. 'Nuff said. Elle Masterson falls for him and I suspect you will, too.

As for the wedding, I'm giving all of us the event we've been eagerly awaiting since this series started. Last Chance Ranch foreman Emmett Sterling will finally tie the knot with B and B owner Pam Mulholland! As everyone at the ranch would say if given the opportunity—it's about time!

If this is your first visit to the Sons of Chance series and you're worried that you won't know the bride and groom or the wedding guests, fear not. I promise you can jump into this story and feel right at home. If you've stuck with me from the beginning, though, you may get an extra dose of joy from watching the festivities as Emmett and Pam say "I do."

So bundle up, grab a travel mug of hot cider and come spend the holidays with the gang from the Last Chance Ranch. Everyone's expecting you!

Joyfully yours,

Vicki

Vicki Lewis Thompson

—

Cowboys & Angels

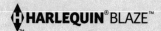

Recycling programs
for this product may
not exist in your area.

ISBN-13: 978-0-373-79779-0

COWBOYS & ANGELS

Printed in U.S.A.

ABOUT THE AUTHOR

New York Times bestselling author Vicki Lewis Thompson's love affair with cowboys started with the Lone Ranger, continued through Maverick and took a turn south of the border with Zorro. She views cowboys as the Western version of knights in shining armor—rugged men who value honor, honesty and hard work. Fortunately for her, she lives in the Arizona desert, where broad-shouldered, lean-hipped cowboys abound. Blessed with such an abundance of inspiration, she only hopes that she can do them justice. Visit her website, www.vickilewisthompson.com.

Books by Vicki Lewis Thompson

HARLEQUIN BLAZE
544—WANTED!*
550—AMBUSHED!*
556—CLAIMED!*
618—SHOULD'VE BEEN A COWBOY*
624—COWBOY UP*
630—COWBOYS LIKE US*
651—MERRY CHRISTMAS, BABY*
    "It's Christmas, Cowboy!"
687—LONG ROAD HOME*
693—LEAD ME HOME*
699—FEELS LIKE HOME*
751—I CROSS MY HEART*
755—WILD AT HEART*
759—THE HEART WON'T LIE*

*Sons of Chance

With gratitude to Dana Hopkins for her steady hand on the editorial reins and her most excellent tweets.

Prologue

December 24, 1989
Last Chance Ranch

A WHITE CHRISTMAS was all well and good, but somebody had to shovel the snow off the front porch, and
Archie Chance had appointed himself caretaker of
that chore. His wife, Nelsie, had tried to talk him out
of it, but he was the logical guy for the job. Everyone
else was busy wrapping presents and cooking food.

In the ninth decade of his life, Archie could still
wield a mean shovel, whether he was mucking out a
stall or clearing a path through the snow. He rather
enjoyed both jobs.

After bundling up in a sheepskin jacket, earmuffs
and his Stetson, Archie took a pair of gloves out of his
coat pocket and opened the massive oak door. Yeah,
it was cold out this morning, but he'd endured worse.
Frigid winters were a fact of life in Jackson Hole.

The snow shovel was kept handy by the door all
winter. Archie picked it up, scooped up a load of snow
and was about to throw it over the porch railing when

the ranch foreman, Emmett Sterling, called out to him. The tall cowboy made deep ruts in the snow as he plowed his way from the barn up to the house.

Archie emptied the shovel and leaned on it as he watched Emmett approach. "Nelsie called down to the barn, didn't she?" The phone connection to the barn was a recent addition, and right now Archie didn't care for it.

"She might've."

Archie blew out a breath, which created a substantial cloud in the air. "Look, I'll be fine out here. My back hasn't bothered me in quite a while."

"And Nelsie wants to keep it that way." Snow crunched under the tall cowboy's boots as he mounted the steps. "Especially seeing as how it's Christmas tomorrow. She doesn't want you putting your back out right before the big day. Can't say I blame her."

Archie considered his options. He was Emmett's boss, so he could refuse to turn over the shovel. But Emmett had interrupted his own chores in the barn to come up here and help, so sending him back down would mean more wasted time.

Archie also realized that if he insisted on shoveling and happened to reinjure his back, he'd look like a stubborn jackass. Nelsie would be ticked off, and making her mad wouldn't help the celebration of Christmas any.

"Much as I hate to admit it, you make a good point, Emmett." With a sigh of resignation, Archie relinquished the shovel.

"I'd be obliged if you'd hang around and keep me company," Emmett said. "Conversation makes the job go faster."

"Be glad to." Archie laughed. "Nothing wrong with my jawbone." As he brushed the snow off the porch railing and leaned against it, he thought about the kindness inherent in Emmett's invitation, as if he knew Archie had come outside partly to enjoy the crisp winter air. Emmett was less than half Archie's age, but he understood people better than most anybody Archie knew.

"I hope you don't fault Nelsie for calling me," Emmett said as he tossed snow over the railing. "She just cares about you, is all."

"I know that. She's a good woman, and I'm a lucky man to have someone like her fussing over me. It's just…"

"You don't want to be fussed over." Emmett dumped more snow into the yard.

"You got that right. And I like to think I can do everything the same as I always did. She knows I'm touchy that way, and she doesn't nag me. Not much, anyway."

"You said it yourself, Archie. She's a good woman, and you're a lucky man."

Archie heard the note of longing in Emmett's voice. Emmett's wife, Jeri, had decided ranch life didn't suit her and had divorced Emmett a couple of years ago. She'd taken their young daughter, Emily, back to California with her.

Although Emmett could have fought that, he hadn't. Instead, he made do with sporadic visits from Emily. Archie thought it was a shame the marriage hadn't worked out. Emmett would have made a good family man.

Archie didn't get too many opportunities to talk

privately with Emmett, so he decided to make use of this one. "You can tell me to mind my own business, but I can't help wondering. Have you ever thought of remarrying?"

"Nope." Emmett kept shoveling.

"Sorry if that was too personal."

"It wasn't." Emmett propped the shovel on the porch floor and leaned on it while he looked over at Archie. "I didn't mean to sound like it was. I just don't have any interest in marrying again."

"Why not?"

Emmett paused, as if considering his answer. "Mostly it's about Emily. All my spare cash goes to my daughter, and any woman I hooked up with would rightly conclude she came second to Emily. Not many would accept that, and if they wanted to have children, what then? I wouldn't start a new family when I still have Emily to think of."

"The right woman would understand."

Emmett smiled. "Maybe. But if that's so, I haven't found her yet."

"Well, I hope you keep looking."

"I hate to disappoint you, Archie, but I'm not looking. The kind of woman who would be happy with a cowpoke in my situation is a rare breed. I seriously doubt I'll ever marry again."

1

CRAMMED INTO THE small backseat of Watkins's king cab, Trey Wheeler thought about the wedding he would soon be a part of. He'd worked as a horse trainer at the Last Chance Ranch for a few months, so he didn't know the groom, Emmett Sterling, all that well. But Trey could tell the ranch foreman was majorly stressed about his upcoming nuptials.

His fiancée, Pam Mulholland, ran a B and B down the road from the Last Chance. She seemed like a nice lady, but when it came to this wedding, she wasn't making things easy on Emmett. Even a newcomer like Trey could see that.

Pam was wealthy and Emmett was not. Although Emmett was crazy about Pam, he'd allowed their financial differences to keep him from proposing until the previous summer, when a shyster had blown into town and shown interest in Pam. Emmett had thought it prudent to take her off the market before he ended up losing her forever.

But Pam, who'd been previously married to a cheating bastard, wanted the wedding of the century this time, and she'd reserved the entire Serenity Ski Lodge in Jackson Hole for a Christmas-themed celebration. Trey was thrilled because Pam had hired him to play guitar for the ceremony along with Watkins, a seasoned ranch hand and the husband of Mary Lou Simms, the ranch's cook. Trey had caught a ride up to the Serenity resort with Watkins and Mary Lou, who were as eager for several days of celebrating as everyone else. Everyone, that was, except the groom.

Trey edged his guitar case aside and leaned toward the front seat as they navigated the snowy road leading to the resort. "Do you think there's a chance Emmett will bail and ruin everything?"

"No," Mary Lou said. She'd tamed her flyaway gray hair under a furry hat. "I've known Emmett Sterling for a lot of years, and he's considerate. He might not like this operation, but it's what Pam wants, and he loves her."

"That's a fact," Watkins agreed. "And the Chance family has gone to some trouble to hire temporary help so we could all get up here and stay a couple of days after the wedding. Emmett wouldn't mess with that kind of generosity."

"I hope not." Trey looked out at the snowy landscape. "I know how much everybody's looking forward to this, including me."

Watkins grinned as he glanced in the rearview mirror. "You gonna try skiing, cowboy?"

"You know, I might. I mean, thanks to Pam, it's free, so why not?"

"That's what I'm thinking," Watkins said. "At least the bunny slope, right, Lou-Lou?"

"At least. I used to be pretty good, but I haven't skied in years. I hope it's like riding a bike and it'll all come back to me once I suit up."

Watkins sent her a fond glance. "I can't wait to see you all decked out. I'll bet you'll look great in goggles."

Mary Lou laughed. "No, I won't, you old flatterer, but I appreciate the thought."

Trey got a kick out of those two. They were both in their fifties, and Watkins had been after Mary Lou for years. She'd resisted the idea of tying the knot until about eighteen months ago, but now that they were married, they both seemed deliriously happy. It was very cute.

The truck approached a curve, and Trey sucked in a breath, as he always did when he came to this part of the road.

"You okay back there?" Watkins glanced in the rearview mirror again.

"Yeah. This is where I had my accident last spring. It always gets to me a little bit."

"I'm sure it does." Mary Lou looked back at him, her gaze sympathetic. "You could've died."

"I would've died, if that woman hadn't come along." *His angel.* For the millionth time, he asked himself why she'd come to his rescue and then left before he could thank her.

He'd been heartbroken after getting a Dear John letter from Cassie, who'd moved back east to attend law school and had fallen for someone there. In the predawn hours, he'd lost control of his Jeep on this curve. Pure misery had kept him from fastening his seat belt, so when the Jeep flipped, he'd been thrown into a snowdrift.

As cold as it had been that morning, he could easily have died from exposure. But his angel had shown up, pulled him out of the snow, taken him to the hospital and left. In his dazed state, he only remembered a halo of blond hair, blue eyes and a soft voice. He also thought she'd come to his hospital room once to check on him, but he'd been really out of it and might have dreamed that.

After he'd recovered, he'd tried unsuccessfully to find out her name. His search had yielded nothing. If she'd given it to the hospital personnel, it had disappeared somehow. Nobody could help him.

Without a name, his chances of finding her dropped considerably. He couldn't even describe her very well, other than her blond hair and blue eyes. Lots of women in the Jackson Hole area had blond hair and blue eyes. She also might have been a tourist, which meant she could live anywhere. People from all over the world visited Jackson Hole.

He wasn't even sure he'd recognize her if he saw her on the street. But her voice haunted his dreams, and he thought he might know the sound of it if he heard it again. More than once he'd stopped a blonde walking down the sidewalk in Jackson and asked her something lame, like directions to the nearest burger joint, so he could listen to her voice. None of them had sounded like his angel.

He'd begun to think she might have been an honest-to-God angel instead of a real woman. He didn't really believe in such things, but that would explain her sudden appearance at his hour of need and why she'd vanished into thin air after rescuing him. Still, he kept looking and listening, hoping that he'd meet her again so he could express his gratitude.

In the meantime, because he owed his life to her, he'd wanted to do something to commemorate her rescue. She might be a caring woman who didn't want to be identified, or she might be a spirit sent down from heaven. In either case, she was his angel.

After much thought, he'd chosen to have an angel's wing tattooed on his left biceps in her honor. Whenever he looked at it, he was reminded that he was one lucky son of a bitch to be alive. In the months that had followed the accident, he'd also realized that Cassie had not been worth dying for. He was ready to move on. Unfortunately, the woman who had made that epiphany possible had vanished without a trace.

ELLE MASTERSON LOOKED forward to having the Last Chance Ranch folks at Serenity for a long weekend while the foreman and his lady got hitched. She'd been warned by management that these would not be experienced skiers, but teaching beginners was her first love. With no other guests to take care of, she'd build her schedule around whatever they wanted, beginning first thing in the morning.

Before then, she needed to finish her Christmas shopping. Rather than head into Jackson, she'd decided to see if she could find something for her favorite cousin in the Serenity resort gift shop. The items were pricey, but she'd get an employee discount.

The shop wasn't busy. The only customer was a tall cowboy, probably part of the Last Chance bunch,

who had his back to her as he glanced through a se-
lection of postcards on a rack near the door. Samantha, a fun-loving, curvaceous redhead, stood behind
the jewelry counter at the far end of the store, and Elle
headed in that direction.

"Hey, Elle! What's up?" Samantha seemed eager
for company.

"I need something pretty for my cousin Jill. A necklace, maybe. She likes turquoise, but she also likes
nature-themed stuff, like wolves and—"

"My God, it's you! I recognize your voice!"

She whirled toward the speaker. The tall cowboy
who'd been shopping for postcards stood at the end
of the jewelry counter staring at her as if he'd seen a
ghost. One glance into his brown eyes and she knew
why.

Trey Wheeler looked completely recovered and perfectly healthy. He also was as drop-dead gorgeous as
she'd remembered. Like most cowboys, he wore his
hat indoors, the brim pulled down a bit so it shadowed
his eyes and gave him an air of mystery. He'd also left
on his sheepskin jacket, but he'd unbuttoned it, which
provided a glimpse of his physique.

The guy was built like a defensive end—slim hips,
broad shoulders, powerful chest. She wondered if he
was still hung up on Cassie, the woman he'd called
out for at the hospital, the woman he'd begged not to
leave him.

He swallowed. "So you're real, after all." His voice
was husky with emotion.

"Did you think I wasn't?" Then she considered
what shape he'd been in after the accident. He'd suf-

fered from exposure and a concussion. He might have thought she was a hallucination.

Samantha spoke up from behind the counter. "Could one of you fill me in? Sounds like there's a story here."

Elle turned to her. "This gentleman flipped his Jeep into a snowbank last April, and I took him to the hospital."

"Then you disappeared," Trey added. "I've been searching for you ever since. Where did you go?"

"Argentina."

His eyebrows shot up. "You live there?"

"Six months out of the year, starting in April. Then I'm here for six months. I'm a ski instructor."

He nodded slowly, as if fitting the pieces together. "That explains why I didn't run into you around town. But I wish you'd left your name and contact information. You saved my life. I wanted to show my appreciation for that."

"Wow, Elle." Samantha gazed at her. "You're just like the Lone Ranger!"

"My thoughts exactly." Trey seemed to have recovered his poise. He walked forward and held out his hand. "But now that you're unmasked, allow me to introduce myself."

She knew his name, but didn't want him to know that she knew, so she kept quiet.

"I'm Trey Wheeler, horse trainer out at the Last Chance, and I'm exceedingly grateful for what you did."

She grasped his large hand. His grip was firm, warm, and…sexy. Tingles of awareness shot through her. "You're welcome. I'm glad I happened along."

She tried to extract her hand, but he held it captive as he smiled down at her. "Not so fast. I still don't know your name."

"Elle Masterson." The continued physical contact jacked up her heart rate.

"Nice to meet you at last, Elle. Buying you dinner doesn't seem like much of a payback, but it's a beginning. Are you busy tonight?"

She scrambled to get her bearings. Trey Wheeler was a fast mover. She should have anticipated such an invitation, but she hadn't. "Sorry, but I make it a policy not to date resort guests." She smiled to take the sting out of the rejection.

"I get that, but this isn't a date. It's a thank-you dinner for saving my life. That's significantly more important than a date."

"So you'll take me to dinner and consider your obligation to me fully satisfied?"

He grinned. "I didn't say that."

Her heartbeat ratcheted up another notch. He had a killer smile going on, and he was employing it to maximum effect. He seemed determined to charm her, and he was accomplishing his goal.

But she followed her personal rule about not dating guests for many reasons. All sorts of complications could arise, including getting fired for unprofessional conduct. Every resort she'd worked for had agreed it was a good policy, although some were more relaxed about the issue than others.

And even if she didn't have a strict policy against dating guests, she'd be wary of dating this one. Catching a guy on the rebound wasn't her idea of fun. She took a deep breath. "I'm sorry, Trey, but dinner isn't a good idea. I understand that you want to thank me in some way, but anyone would have done the same under similar circumstances. Your gratitude is very sweet, but you don't owe me for doing the right thing."

"I think I do, but if dinner won't work, I'll come up with something else."

"No, really. That's unnecessary. Knowing that you're all recovered is enough of a reward for me."

His brown gaze was warm as it swept over her. "I admire your modesty, but this is important to me, and I'm not the kind of man to just let it go. You'll be hearing from me. See you later, Elle." He touched the brim of his hat and walked out of the shop.

She stared after him, her pulse hopping around like a Mexican jumping bean.

"You should have accepted his invitation to dinner," Samantha said.

Elle turned. "You know I don't believe in getting cozy with a guest."

"Yeah, but he has a point about the special circumstances. Besides, not many guests look like him. He's one hot cowboy. I say he's worthy of a little rule-bending."

"Let's think about this for a minute, Sam. He's not simply a guest. He works at a ranch in the area, which means he won't be completely gone come Tuesday afternoon."

"Even better! Then he'll stop being the kind of conflict of interest that bothers you so much."

"No, but..." Elle felt ridiculous putting her reservations about Trey into words. She'd sound paranoid, or at least presumptuous. She didn't know him at all, so she couldn't predict how he'd behave in a relationship.

Yet she'd heard his heartbroken plea to Cassie, obviously his former lover. Cassie might be old news by now, but Trey didn't strike her as the type who'd be fine with dating a woman who spent half the year in Argentina. He seemed too intense for a casual affair.

Casual affairs were all she allowed herself because she had such a great life following the snow. She didn't want to tie herself down to one place or one man. Not yet, anyway.

Maybe in a few years she'd grow tired of the traveling. At that point, someone like Trey would be a possibility. But he wasn't right for her now, no matter how fast her heart beat when he was near.

Samantha frowned in obvious disapproval. "I know what it means when you tighten your jaw. You're going to reject this yummy man's advances, aren't you?"

Elle consciously relaxed her jaw and smiled at Sam. "Yep. But you're welcome to him, if he appeals to you that much."

"Oh, he does, but I don't stand a chance. He only has eyes for you."

"That's silly."

"No, it's incredibly romantic. Did you hear what he said? He recognized your *voice*. That means he carried the sound of your voice around in his head for months while he searched for you. The memory of you *haunted* him. How great is that?"

Elle rolled her eyes. "You really should ask him out. You're obviously into his brand of drama."

"You should be, too. A Prince Charming like him doesn't come along every day of the week. You may look back on this later and realize you screwed up a golden opportunity."

"Maybe I will, Sam, but the timing is way off." She gazed at her friend. "He may be a prince, but I'm not ready for a fairy-tale ending."

2

TREY ENJOYED A rowdy dinner with everyone from the Last Chance, including the prospective bride and groom. Once Trey understood the layout of the resort, he realized that his spur-of-the-moment invitation to Elle might have been impractical. The formal dining room had been appropriated for Last Chance people, which left the coffee shop and the bar for private meals. Neither of those places suited Trey's image of treating Elle to a special dining experience.

During dinner, the hotel manager passed around sign-up sheets for resort activities. Trey had never skied a day in his life, but he signed up for lessons when he saw that Elle was listed as one of the instructors.

For eight months she'd been a mystery woman he couldn't forget, but other than her voice, her eyes and that halo of blond hair, he'd known nothing about her. She could have been a teenager or a senior citizen, short or tall, plump or skinny, plain or pretty.

And now he knew. She took his breath away. How amazing to think that Pam and Emmett's wedding had brought him face-to-face with Elle Masterson, his angel. Hearing her voice had been a jolt. Seeing her standing there in all her glory had made him feel as if Christmas had come early this year.

Oh, yeah, he wanted to get to know her better. He thought she might want the same thing. Her blue eyes had sparkled with interest when she'd looked at him, so even though she'd thrown up roadblocks, he would persevere. That flash of sexual attraction had been decidedly mutual.

He understood why she'd be wary of getting involved with a resort guest, but he'd only be in that category for a few days. If he laid the groundwork now, he could build on it later, when he was no longer a guest.

Something had clicked for him the moment he'd rounded that corner in the gift shop and laid eyes on her. She might think coincidence had made her drive past where he'd swerved off the road, but now that they'd met, he wouldn't call it coincidence. He'd call it destiny.

After dinner, he and Watkins checked out the wedding ceremony venue, a large space with exposed beams and warm wood paneling. In daylight, when the ceremony would take place, the curtained windows would look out on pines and ski slopes. The candlelit reception in the evening was scheduled for the adjoining ballroom. Trey and Watkins would play then, too.

"It'll be real nice," Watkins said, looking around the room where the wedding would take place. "The acoustics should be decent, too. I'm glad they carpeted the floor."

"Did you want to practice tonight?"

"Nah, let's not." Watkins smoothed his handlebar

mustache. "There's a country-and-western band play-ing in the bar, and Mary Lou wants to dance. She doesn't get to do that whenever I'm playing, so this will be a treat for both of us. She's probably already in the bar ready to boot scoot."

"Before you go, I wanted to tell you something."

Watkins, who was a good six inches shorter than Trey and at least fifty pounds heavier, glanced up at him. "What's that, son?"

Trey liked that Watkins called him "son." Trey's folks were both gone, his mom from cancer and his dad in an oil rig accident. Although Trey had come to grips with not having living parents, he reveled in the family atmosphere of the Last Chance and ap-preciated how Watkins and Mary Lou had taken him under their wing.

"I've found her," he said. "My angel. She works at the resort."

"No kidding!"

"She's one of the ski instructors, and her name is Elle Masterson."

"Well, I'll be." Watkins stroked his mustache again. "What's she like?"

"Perfect."

"Hold on there, cowboy. No woman's perfect. You know how I feel about Lou-Lou, but I'd be the first to admit she's not perfect. Don't go setting some lady on a pedestal. You'll regret it."

"You're right." Privately, Trey didn't think so. "But Elle is darned close. And she likes me. I can tell she does."

"Then why didn't she identify herself when she

hauled your ass to the hospital? Something's not adding up here."

"I know, and I mean to get to the bottom of that. But the main issue is her principles. She doesn't believe resort employees should get involved with resort guests."

Watkins nodded. "She must be a sensible woman, then. You can't have that kind of thing in a fancy establishment like this. You need to respect her wishes on that."

"I will. And I do. But don't you think this is a special case? She saved my life. And she likes me. I hate to waste time on rules and regulations in this situation."

Watkins smiled. "You're talking about four days, right?"

"Well, yeah, but—"

"It's not a long time, son. I know at your age it seems forever, but trust me, those four days will go by fast."

"I suppose." Once again, Trey didn't agree with Watkins. After eight months of searching for his mystery woman, he'd finally found her, and she was wonderful. He was eager to explore the possibilities, and they'd both be staying under the same roof, so to speak. He couldn't imagine how time spent that way would go by fast.

"You don't believe me." Watkins clapped a hand on his shoulder. "That's okay. But don't go back to your room and stare at the ceiling all night. Get your guitar and come down for a drink. I know these guys who are playing, and they'd probably let you sit in on a set or two. It'll be good practice."

"Sure, why not?" Given that his hands were tied when it came to Elle, he couldn't think of a better way to spend the evening.

AFTER A QUICK supper in the employees' dining room, Elle climbed the stairs to her room on the second floor of the staff's quarters. A printout of the next day's schedule had been left on her desk, and she picked it up. No big surprise, Trey had registered for her group lesson first thing in the morning.

She was one of three ski instructors employed by Serenity, but Annalise had been given the weekend off because these guests wouldn't need advanced lessons. Elle and her colleague Jared could handle the Last Chance group, who were mostly all beginners.

Switching Trey to Jared's group would make an issue out of the situation, so she'd leave the schedule as it was. But she had to smile when she noticed that Jared had all women except for a guy named Watkins, and she had all men.

Besides Trey, Elle would be working with Alex Keller, Nash Bledsoe, Jeb Branford and two of the Chance brothers, Gabe and Nick. Elle hadn't met any of them, although she certainly recognized the names of the Chance boys. There was a third brother, Jack, but apparently he wasn't into skiing lessons.

All the men except Alex Keller had checked the beginner box on the sign-up sheet. Alex had checked the box indicating he had some experience, which meant he might be willing to help the others. All in all, it should be a fun morning. She loved taking nonskiers and turning them into enthusiastic fans of the sport.

As she considered whether to hit the sack early

to be ready for tomorrow's activities, her cell phone chimed. For some reason, Amy, the bartender on duty tonight, was calling her. Elle picked up her phone. "Hey, Amy."

"Unless you're in your jammies already, you should get yourself down here."

"I was almost in my jammies. What's happening?"

"One of the guys from the Last Chance is performing with the band and he is *hot*. I know you're a country fan. Come down and I'll put you to work behind the bar so you'll have an excuse to hang around."

Elle had become enamored of country music in the past year, and hearing it live was always a treat. Besides, she didn't feel tired enough to go to bed yet. "Thanks, I'll be right there." Disconnecting the phone, she ran a comb through her hair, reapplied her lipstick, popped a mint and grabbed her room key. She'd helped Amy behind the bar a few times before, and she liked the job.

On her way downstairs, she breathed in the scent of Christmas. Serenity went all-out this time of year, and she liked spending the holidays here. Each guest room door had its own fresh wreath, complete with a couple of cinnamon sticks tucked into a big red bow.

Staff members didn't get wreaths, but they were all given small trees to decorate. Hers was sitting in a corner of her room, waiting for her to get busy with lights and ornaments. Until she did, she could enjoy the fifteen-foot blue spruce in the lobby, which sparkled with lights and elegant glass balls. Pine boughs, pinecones and festive ribbons decorated the check-in desk.

The bar opened off the lobby, so the music drifted

toward her as she walked past the Christmas tree toward the heavy double doors inset with stained glass.
Someone was singing in a husky baritone that tickled
her nerve endings.

"Going in to hear our new star?" called Ralph from
the front desk.

"Yeah, I'm told he's pretty good. Amy is letting me
help behind the bar."

Ralph laughed. "Have fun. The women tell me he
looks pretty good, too."

"I'm just here for the music, Ralph."

"That's what they all say."

As Elle grasped the brass handle and opened the
door, she had a premonition about who this sexy country singer might be, but she discounted it. The universe
wouldn't be so generous as to give the bodacious Trey
Wheeler a great singing voice, too.

Obviously the universe was exactly that generous.
Sitting on a stool in front of the mike, strumming his
guitar and crooning a solo love song, was the man
she was determined to avoid, the man every woman
in the room was fixated on. The rest of the band was
silent, not that they would have been noticed if they
had decided to play backup.

Trey's face was shielded by the lowered brim of his
hat, and he seemed completely absorbed in his music.
He cradled the guitar in his lap. One booted foot rested
on the floor and the other was propped on a rung of
the stool. His supple fingers moved up and down the
guitar's polished neck in a sensuous dance as his voice
flowed over her, intimate as a caress.

Lost in a daze of feminine appreciation, she stood
motionless in the doorway. The atmosphere in the

room was electric. Nobody laughed. No glasses clinked. Trey had them all in the palm of his hand.

Then he looked up, as if he'd sensed her come in, and he gazed straight into her eyes.

Her breath caught. He was no longer singing to some unidentified lover. He was singing to her. The passionate lyrics spilled from his lips with such longing that she took a step closer. His slow smile told her he'd noticed, and she halted, embarrassed by how he'd hypnotized her.

Mercifully, the song ended before Elle lost all sense of propriety. After the raucous applause died down, Trey stepped back and the band launched into a lively swing tune. Another guitarist moved up to the mike to belt out the lyrics, and Elle hurried over to the bar.

Amy, who wore her dark hair piled on top of her head, grinned at her. "Told you."

"Yes, ma'am, you did." Elle lifted the hinged part of the bar and scooted inside. "The thing is, I kind of know him already."

"You *do?* Then you get dibs. But if you don't want him, then— Oh, crap. I see orders coming in. We'll talk later."

The next twenty minutes were a flurry of drink orders and washing glasses. But at the first lull, Amy brought up the subject immediately. "So how do you know him? Please tell me he's an old family friend and you think of him like a brother."

"I wish." Elle told her about last spring's incident involving Trey, and their chance meeting in the gift shop today.

"My God, that means he wrote that song about you! He introduced it by saying he'd been rescued by an angel. That totally explains why he focused on you for the last part of the song."

"He wrote it about me?" Elle's cheeks warmed. "That's sort of…"

"Romantic. It's romantic, Elle. Seems like you hooked him good by going all mystery woman on him for eight months. I envy the hell out of you. He's mighty fine."

"I wasn't trying to hook him."

"You did, anyway. Don't look now, but he's coming over here and he looks determined."

Elle turned, and sure enough, Trey was striding toward the bar carrying his guitar case. Her breath hitched. "Maybe he wants a drink."

"I think he wants you, *chica.*"

Elle had to admit Amy was probably right. The heat in Trey's eyes was unmistakable.

He set down his guitar case and leaned on the bar. "I didn't know you'd be here, Elle."

"Amy needed some help."

Amy glanced away, but was unsuccessful at muffling a snort of laughter.

"Hmm." He didn't appear to be buying that. "I'm glad you did, especially because I happened to be singing your song."

"I…I didn't realize you were a musician." Her resistance to this gorgeous man was fading fast. No one had ever written a song about her. She liked to think she wasn't susceptible to such romantic gestures, but the butterflies in her stomach signaled otherwise.

"Could we go somewhere and talk?"

"You're not going to play anymore?"

He shook his head. "That's enough for tonight."

"Amy might need me to stay."

"Nope," Amy said. "Thanks for the help, but I can handle it."

Elle took a deep breath. "Okay, then. We can go out in the lobby. There are some comfy chairs in front of the fire."

He seemed about to comment on that suggestion, but then he didn't. "All right. Lead the way." But the minute they were out the door, he put a hand on her arm. "I'd rather go somewhere more private than the lobby."

She turned and looked into his eyes. That was a big mistake. The intensity reflected there, combined with the lingering effects of his song, tempted her beyond reason. She shouldn't surrender to his magnetism, but resisting it was proving difficult.

He lowered his voice. "My room?"

She shook her head. "Sorry."

His gaze sharpened. "Then tell me where I can find you."

Dear God, she was considering the possibility of inviting him to *her* room. She shouldn't do that. She really shouldn't. But if they were alone, she could explain why she didn't want to get involved with him. She could mention his ravings about Cassie.

He was right that they needed privacy for that kind of conversation, and the options were few. They couldn't very well take a walk in subzero temperatures. But if he came to her room, they could speak freely and clear the air once and for all.

Yeah, right. Their meeting might go that way, but if she didn't keep a tight rein on her libido, it might go another way, too. He was one potent cowboy. The thought of being along with him made her quiver.

"Please, Elle," he murmured. "We have a connection, you and I. We need to talk about it, figure a few things out. At least I do."

She let out a breath. If they didn't settle this now, it would hang over them all weekend. "Okay. My room, then. But we shouldn't be seen going there together." She quickly gave him directions.

"I'll drop off my guitar and be there in a few minutes."

She nodded. Heart racing, she hurried out of the lobby and down the hall toward the staff quarters. This was insanity, but then, Trey was making her insane—insane enough to risk being alone with him.

Nothing had to happen if she maintained control. That might be easier said than done, though. She was playing with fire when it came to an emotional man like Trey. Adrenaline fueled her steps as she ran up the stairs.

Once in her room, she straightened up the place, although judging from Trey's intense focus, he wouldn't care if the room was trashed. She cared, though. She'd been a military brat, and her parents' neat-freak habits were deeply ingrained. Order and discipline had been her watchwords since childhood.

Trey's sentimental approach to life both fascinated and frightened her. His ability to stir an emotional response in her was a warning signal that he could disrupt her carefully managed existence. But he couldn't knock her off-kilter unless she allowed it. So she'd just have to stay in command of the situation.

3

WHEN TREY HAD packed for the weekend, he'd used his trusty duffel, as always. Maybe, just maybe, he had some condoms tucked in a side pocket of that duffel. He probably shouldn't be thinking about that. He shouldn't, but he was.

The whole time he'd been talking with Elle in the lobby, she'd given off sparks. If he had to guess, he'd say she was affected by his song about her. That was okay with him. He'd written it months ago as an expression of joy and gratitude, but it seemed as if everything he wrote came out sounding like a love song in the end.

He sensed that her argument against dating him wasn't as strong as it had been this afternoon. The tide had turned in his favor, and if, in the privacy of her room, the heat started building…well, he didn't want to be without the means to follow through. A condom didn't take up much room in his pocket, and if he didn't need it, no harm done.

He might not find a stash in his duffel, but it had been his traveling companion during his relationship with Cassie. Chances were good some were still in there. Funny how the thought of Cassie didn't bother him anymore. She'd never have been happy with a cowboy who planned to stay in Wyoming for the duration.

The aroma of fresh pine greeted him as he fit the key card into the door to his room. At some point he'd track down Pam Mulholland and thank her for treating everyone to a weekend at this plush resort. He'd fully expected to bunk with someone at the very least, but Pam had reserved separate rooms for each of them. What a luxury.

Pulling his duffel from the closet, he checked the side pocket and hit pay dirt. He took one condom and left the rest. Then he reviewed the directions she'd given him.

His hat would only be in the way, so he left it in his room. Once he was in the hallway again, he decided that maybe he should head toward the staff quarters by a roundabout route. If anyone questioned him, he'd pretend to be lost. If she'd established a policy of not dating guests, she wouldn't want anyone to know she'd invited him to her room.

In the end, he managed to actually get lost. Feeling like an idiot, he retraced his steps and by a stroke of luck didn't encounter anyone as he roamed the halls. Eventually he found her room and rapped softly.

She opened the door dressed in the same outfit she'd had on when they'd parted. Apparently, she hadn't decided to slip into something more comfortable. He had no idea how this meeting would go, but at least they'd be able to talk without any danger of being overheard.

"I'd about given up on you." She scanned the hall-way before whisking him inside.

"I got lost." He hated admitting it, but that was better than letting her think he'd dillydallied around.

"Really?" She closed the door and leaned against it. Her breathing seemed a little fast. "My directions were pretty straightforward."

"They were, but I wanted to confuse anyone who might see me walking the halls, so I took a different route and ended up confusing myself, too." He wasn't breathing normally, either. Being alone with her in a room with a bed was messing with him.

She looked amazing. He hadn't paid much attention to what she had on before, but now he was intensely interested. She wore black jeggings and cute little boots that were fashionable but useless. A light blue sweater with a V neck clung to her breasts. Gazing at her caused his groin to tighten.

"So you deliberately tried to keep your destination a secret?"

"Yeah."

"Thank you." Her expression softened. "I appreciate that."

"Judging from what you said earlier, you wouldn't want anyone to know I'm here."

She nodded. "But I'm not as worried about that as I am about…other things."

"Like what?" She was still leaning against the door and he was a good ten feet away, his back to her curtained window. He cut the space between them in half and would have moved even closer, but she put up her hand like a traffic cop.

"Hold it right there, cowboy. You were right when you said we need to talk."

He couldn't help smiling. "We do, but I'd rather not have to shout."

She mirrored his smile. "It's a small room. You were hardly within shouting distance. Just stay right there for now, okay?"

He did. Never let it be said that he forced his attention on a woman. Her eyes told him she was as revved up by their proximity as he was, but he'd let the situation unfold naturally.

Her chest heaved, which made her breasts quiver. "You probably can tell that I'm attracted to you."

"God, I hope so. Otherwise I've lost my ability to recognize interest when I see it." He was gratified when his comment made that flame ignite in her eyes once again. Her lips parted, and she looked so ready for a kiss that he considered ignoring her command to hold his ground.

"We need to talk about Cassie."

That cooled his jets. *"Cassie?"* He couldn't have been more shocked if she'd mentioned ties to the Mafia. "You know her?"

"Not at all, but I came to see you after you were admitted to the hospital, and you kept asking for her. You…uh…begged her not to leave you. You were quite emotional."

Embarrassment washed through him, and he scrubbed a hand over his face as if to erase the color he knew would be there. "She's totally out of my life. At the time when I rolled the Jeep, I was still upset about the breakup, but I'm over her."

"Are you sure about that?"

"Yes. I'm not the kind of guy who would hit on a woman if I was still in love with someone else. I don't use one person to get over another person." How he hated that she'd heard him moaning over Cassie. But he couldn't change what had happened eight months ago, and he really wouldn't want to. The accident had brought them together.

"I'm willing to accept that you're not that kind of man. But that's not the only thing worrying me."

"Then what else?" If there were more obstacles, he hoped to remove them. Discovering whether he and Elle had a chance of building a relationship was his top priority.

"Judging from the way you reacted to breaking up with Cassie, you were deeply in love with her."

"I certainly thought I was, but I've figured out it never would have worked. I've made peace with that." He had a sudden insight. "Is that why you didn't leave any contact information? You thought I was in love with someone else?"

"You *were* in love with someone else."

"I suppose so." He shoved his fingers through his hair. "But I'm not anymore, and I'm extremely interested in you, so I don't understand why we're talking about Cassie."

"I just need to know something. Do you usually get that involved when you're in a relationship?"

He sensed this might be a trap, so he took a moment before he responded. "Sometimes I do, yes." That wasn't quite accurate. He had a tendency to surrender his entire heart to the woman in his life, which left him bruised and battered when the love affair ended. But he didn't know how else to be.

"Getting deeply involved with me wouldn't be a good idea."

"Are you married?" He imagined some Latin lover down in Argentina and wanted to hit something.

"No, and I don't expect to get married for a long, long time."

"That's fine with me, but just for the record, why the repetition of the word *long*? Do you have something against marriage?"

She pointed a finger at him. "See? That's what worries me. I'll bet you're looking for happily ever after."

"Eventually, yeah. What's the matter with that?"

"Not a thing, except…well, I'm just not into that routine."

"Okay."

"I'm looking for 'happy right now.'"

He desperately wanted to touch her. If he could kiss her, this conversation would be unnecessary. She was worrying about things that wouldn't matter for quite a while. When April arrived, they could deal with this issue. Talking about it tonight was a waste of valuable time. "I can work with happy right now."

"You were awfully quick to say that, Trey. I'm not convinced you mean it, especially if you've been thinking about me for months and you even wrote a song about me."

He gazed into her blue eyes and curbed his frustration. Maybe she had a point. Now that he'd discovered that his angel was a beautiful woman, he could be guilty of romanticizing the connection between them and falling in love with the idea of her. Yeah, that sounded like something he'd do.

Blowing out a breath, he shoved his hands in his

pockets so he wouldn't forget himself and reach for her. "It's possible I've attached too much meaning to this chance encounter because of Pam and Emmett's wedding after what happened last spring. But damn it, when a gorgeous woman appears out of nowhere and saves your life, that's gonna make an impression."

"You were delirious. I doubt you saw me all that clearly. You couldn't have known how I looked."

"That's true. I've thought about how dazed and confused I must have been. You could have been seventy-five and missing all your teeth and I wouldn't have known the difference."

She smiled at that.

"But you seemed like some sort of angel with your halo of blond hair, which was lit up somehow."

"From the headlights of my truck, no doubt."

"Probably. I also remembered your beautiful blue eyes, which are as beautiful as I thought they were, by the way."

"Thanks." Her cheeks turned pink.

"But I especially remembered your voice—soft, caring, soothing. I'm a musician, so sound means a lot to me. Your voice, which is also sexy as hell, has been part of many dreams these past few months."

The color in her cheeks darkened. "Oh."

"Now let me ask you something."

"Fair enough."

"Did you ever think of me after that?"

She met his gaze, even though she continued to blush furiously. "Yes."

"Often?"

"Often enough." She drew a quivering breath. "But that whole bit about Cassie made me decide you were too intense for me, so I thought it was better that we'd lost touch."

"And now?" He probably shouldn't have asked that, but the gleam in her eyes made him bolder.

"Oh, Trey. You do turn me on, but I'm so afraid that—"

"Don't be afraid." He pulled her into his arms and lowered his head. He was done talking. "Don't ever be afraid of me."

KNOWING FULL WELL that she was doing *exactly* what she'd vowed not to, Elle gave up the fight. But he was so appealing, so determined, and…oh, dear God, the man could kiss. His mouth covered hers gently at first as he settled in with velvet pressure that was just enough to make her want more. Pulse racing, she cupped the back of his head and parted her lips, inviting him to take as many liberties as he wanted.

And he obviously wanted. He deepened the kiss with a sureness that made her gasp. There would be no retreat now. She'd planned to stay in control, but that plan was scrapped the moment she surrendered to the thrust of his tongue. When he splayed his fingers over her bottom and pulled her against his rigid cock, she moaned in excitement.

Clothes became the enemy. She tugged at the snaps of his Western shirt, needing to touch him without any barrier. His breathing roughened when she slid her palms up the furred planes of his muscular chest.

Lifting his mouth a fraction from hers, he chuckled. "I'll take that as a green light."

"Extremely green." She reached for his belt buckle. "I want you naked and I want you now."

"That means we have matching goals." Returning to that most excellent kiss, he slid a hand under her sweater and unfastened her bra with one quick movement.

Things progressed quickly after that. His ability to kiss was matched by his talent for ridding her of her clothes. She completely lost track of her mission to unbuckle his belt.

A girl could be forgiven for being distracted when a hot cowboy expertly slipped off her sweater and put his mouth there…and there…and *there*. She whimpered as he took her nipple between his teeth and tugged. This was going to be good. Very good. She'd worry about the emotional consequences later.

As she adjusted to the wonders of being topless and very well caressed, he moved on, divesting her of her jeggings, panties and boots. After that, well, he *really* took liberties with where he put his clever mouth. And his agile tongue.

Her knees threatened to give way as he drove her insane. "I'm…going to fall…"

"Not on my watch." Scooping her into his arms, he laid her down on the bed and proceeded to finish what he'd started, which meant she had to grab a pillow and press it to her face to muffle the sounds of her heart-pounding orgasm.

The pillow provided some measure of privacy, too. No man had ever produced such an uninhibited reaction in her, and she was a little embarrassed. Here she'd been worried that *he* was too intense, and she was the one bringing all the drama. But wow. Just… *wow*.

The mattress shifted as he climbed off the bed. The

clank of his belt buckle hitting the floor told her that he was completing the task she'd abandoned. One boot thudded to the floor, then another.

Moments later, the mattress dipped again, and he tugged at the pillow. "You under there?"

"Yes."

"Are you hiding?"

"Yes."

"You must be part ostrich, then. They hide just like that, everything exposed but their heads."

That mental image was enough to make her jerk the pillow away and meet his gaze. "Hi."

"Hi, yourself." He slowly combed her hair back from her face.

As she soaked up the warmth from his smile and his amazing brown eyes, she was comforted, but as he continued to look at her, comfort morphed into arousal. Her breath caught.

"What?" He stroked her cheek with one finger. "Why did you gasp like that?"

"I…" Her face felt hot, but the heat didn't stop there. It shot through her, making her ache in a way she hadn't known was possible. "I still want you."

"That's convenient." He cupped her face in one hand and leaned down to feather a kiss over her lips. "I still want you."

"Did you bring any—"

"Yep. Just in case." Foil crinkled, and then he was back, dropping more soft kisses on her mouth as he moved over her.

"Good man." Wrapping her arms around his broad back, she rose to meet him, and they came together as if they'd been doing this forever. No fumbling, no miscues. One sure thrust, and they were locked in an age-old embrace.

"Mmm." His hum of praise vibrated against her mouth.

She couldn't have said it better. He fit her perfectly, his hard cock stretching her just enough to make her want more. She hadn't had a lot of lovers, but none of them had felt so absolutely right.

That scared her more than a little. She wanted this kind of perfection someday, but she wasn't ready for it now. Too late. Trey was here, buried deep inside her, and he had started to move. *Sweet heaven*.

If she'd thought they were a nice combination while stationary, they were a spectacular event when in motion. He began slow and easy, giving her time to catch his rhythm. She didn't need any time. Instinctively, she knew him, knew his moves.

"Open your eyes."

She did, and discovered he was looking down at her as he rocked forward and back, forward and back. Each roll of his hips brought her climax nearer. He made it seem effortless, as if he could love her this way for hours, yet surely he must be struggling to hold back. If so, he gave no indication.

"Your eyes are getting darker," he murmured.

The coil of tension within her tightened another notch as she held his gaze. "That's because…" She gulped. "Because I'm close."

"I know." A flicker in his eyes betrayed his excitement, although his pace never altered. "I can feel it."

"You don't have to hold back."

"But I want to hold back." His breath hitched, but

his strokes remained unhurried. "I want to watch you come."

"What about—" She moaned and clutched his hips. How she wanted this, needed this! "What about you?"

"Later. You first." He pushed forward, putting pressure at the critical spot. Then he slid back and pushed in again.

"I need the pillow." Panting, she struggled to hold back her orgasm. "I need it now."

"Use my hand." He covered her mouth gently.

With that, she erupted in a climax that shook her from head to toe. She clutched his hand and pressed it tight against her mouth. Her hips lifted toward the pleasure, and he continued thrusting. She kept coming, her cries captured in the palm of his hand. At last, her body shaking, she sank back onto the sheet. But little aftershocks continued to roll through her.

"My turn." He moved faster, now. Slipping his hands under her bottom, he held her as if knowing she didn't have the strength to do it herself.

Amazingly, she wasn't finished. His rapid strokes brought her right back to the edge, and when he hurled himself over with a deep groan, she followed with a gasp of surprise. As she clung to him and gulped in air, her dazed mind kept returning to one simple truth. She'd started an affair with Trey Wheeler, and keeping it under control would take all her willpower.

4

TREY HAD A million things he wanted to say to Elle as they lay wrapped in each other's arms, but he chose not to say any of them. Actions spoke louder than words, anyway, and their actions tonight in this bed were shouting about the possibilities ahead of them. He'd let her think on it, and he sure as hell would, too.

Going into this, he'd had high expectations. The reality of making love to her had shot way past those expectations, and he suspected the lovemaking would only get better with time. A relationship was built on more than sexual attraction, and he knew that, so the next step was getting better acquainted somewhere other than in bed.

Tomorrow they'd be together for the skiing lesson, with other folks around. He was glad they'd been to bed first, though, so neither of them had to waste time wondering if and when sex would happen. The *if* part was settled, and the *when* would be every chance they had.

He didn't think he was being egotistical to assume that. She'd responded more enthusiastically than any woman he'd been with. She'd want more of that, and heaven knows he would, too. She was incredible. His body had never felt so energized, so damned complete.

But he held off telling her all those things, especially because she was getting drowsier by the second. He'd wondered earlier if she'd notice his angel wing tattoo once his shirt was off, but she hadn't. Just as well.

He wasn't sure how she'd feel about it, jumpy as she was about commitment. Tattoos were permanent, although they did fade with time. Still, Elle might not like the fact that he planned to carry a reminder of her forever, no matter how their relationship turned out.

He stayed with her until she drifted off to sleep. Then he slipped out of bed, dressed quietly and left her room, locking the door behind him.

As he started down the hall, he saw a woman walking in his direction. There was no escape. As they drew closer to each other, he recognized Amy, the bartender. He had no idea what time it was, but she'd probably just gotten off work and was going to her room.

When they met, she smiled at him. "You look worried."

"I am worried. It's obvious where I've been, and I don't want the word to get out."

"I won't rat on you, if that's what you're concerned about."

"I appreciate that."

"But after the introduction to your song tonight, followed by you and Elle leaving the bar together, I predict you won't keep this liaison a secret very long."

Trey sighed. "I don't want to embarrass her. Apparently she has this ironclad rule, and—"

"It's her rule, and she has the right to break it. I can't speak for everyone, but I won't tease her."

"Thanks. And, listen, I also want to thank you for asking Elle to help you behind the bar tonight. That turned out really well."

Amy laughed. "I can see that it did. FYI, your shirt is buttoned up wrong."

"Oh." Trey glanced down and sure enough, she was right. But he couldn't very well fix it right here in front of her. He'd do that after they parted ways. "Anyway, I hope you weren't slammed with orders after we left."

"I wasn't slammed with orders in the first place." Amy's smile widened. "I didn't really need her help. I told her to get her butt down there so she could listen to a hot cowboy sing with the band."

"Really?"

"Really. She loves her some good country music. I had no idea all this other stuff was going on with you two."

"Huh. So my music did have some effect on her."

"I'd guarantee it. Of course, you were having some effect on all the women in the room. Have you thought of doing anything with that gift?"

"Nah. I love training horses. The life of a professional singer doesn't appeal to me at all. Local stuff is all I care to do."

"Too bad. I know it's competitive, but I think you could make it if you wanted to give it a try."

"That's nice to hear, but it just doesn't interest me."

"All righty, then. Guess I'll be going off to bed. See you tomorrow."

"You bet. And thanks again." Trey continued down the hall. So Elle was susceptible to his music, was she? That was a bonus he hadn't counted on.

Amy thought he should do something with his gift. Apparently, he already had. And he'd continue to use it to charm his angel until she figured out they had something special going on.

CARRYING HER SKIS and poles in a zippered bag in one hand and two clipboards in the other, Elle walked out to the bunny hill a little before nine, the time appointed for the beginner lessons. She prided herself on always being on time, but this morning she'd been more motivated than usual.

Jackson Hole had trotted out one of its famously perfect winter mornings. A cobalt sky arched over pine forests crisscrossed with ski runs. Sunlight turned the snow into a rhinestone-studded carpet.

Elle couldn't imagine a more beautiful setting than this one. She'd bounced out of bed with the kind of energy she'd had as a kid. Breakfast had tasted like gourmet fare, even though it was her usual yogurt and fruit combined with strong coffee.

She had plenty of reservations about letting Trey into her life, but for the short term, he'd made her feel as if she'd spent a day at the spa. Her body hummed with awareness knowing she'd see him very soon.

She was already planning ahead, looking for opportunities for them to be alone so that she could feel his magic hands, taste his exotic kisses and feel the thrust of his...well, yes. Definitely that, too. She got hot thinking about it.

He was scheduled to play for the rehearsal dinner

tonight, but after that…he'd be all hers. She'd had a short conversation with Amy in the employee cafeteria, and Amy had mentioned meeting Trey in the hallway. Amy wouldn't gossip, but she'd warned Elle that Trey's song and his subsequent exit from the bar with Elle would fuel rumors.

Probably. She wasn't going to let worry about fall-out dampen her mood today, though. She'd enjoyed the most thrilling sex of her life last night, and the man responsible for that would be at the bunny hill any minute. A little voice in her head warned her that she was flirting with disaster, and she ignored it.

Jared was already there. Leaning her gear against the side of the ski hut they used as a base of operations, she walked over to him. "Ready for the newbies?"

"Absolutely." With his lean, muscular body, Jared fit the image of a sexy ski instructor. He inspired confidence in those he coached with his brilliant smile, which flashed often in a face tanned by constant exposure to sun reflecting off snow.

Women found him irresistible, but Elle had never heard about any liaisons with guests. She decided to ask him about that. "I know the ladies hit on you all the time. Have you ever…?" She wasn't quite sure how to state it so she wouldn't offend him.

Jared winked at her. "Elle, you know perfectly well that a gentleman doesn't discuss his affairs."

"So you have had them!"

"I didn't say that."

"You didn't have to. If you'd walked the straight and narrow, you would have told me. But you hedged."

Jared studied her with dark eyes that hinted at his

Mediterranean heritage. "Why do I get the idea this isn't an idle question?"

"Because it's not, obviously. I've never done anything like this before, and I want to know how much potential trouble I could cause myself."

"Does this have something to do with the singing cowboy?"

She stared at him. "How did you know it was him?"

"Sweetheart, *everybody* knows."

"They do not." She couldn't believe word had traveled that fast. "You're making that up."

"Nope. The Last Chance crowd is well aware that he searched high and low for you following his accident last spring. Add in his revealing performance at the bar last night and the two of you leaving together, and it doesn't take a genius." He surveyed her. "If I needed any confirmation, all I have to do is look at you. You're bright as a penny that just popped out of the U.S. mint."

Elle groaned. "He's signed up for a lesson this morning, along with five other guys from the ranch. Are you saying they'll all know?"

"It's a safe bet."

"Great. How am I supposed to handle *that?*"

"It won't be a problem."

"How do you know? I think it could be a huge problem. Teasing, innuendoes, stuff like that."

"Obviously, you don't know much about cowboys, Elle. I suppose you wouldn't, because they don't come up here much. You've never had a reason to understand the culture."

"What culture?"

"Cowboys have a code of honor. I'm not saying

all of them do, but it's expected of the Last Chance bunch or they're sent on their way. Those guys might give each other grief, but they would never knowingly embarrass a woman, especially a woman connected to one of their buddies."

"How do you know so much about it?"

Jared smiled. "That's what you learn if you stick around during the summer and hang out at the Spirits and Spurs in Shoshone. You should try it sometime."

"I follow the snow."

"I've heard you say that, but doesn't it get monotonous?"

Elle shrugged. "I'm an army brat. Staying in one place all the time is what would get monotonous for me. Besides, skiing is what I do."

"It's what I do, too, but I take a break in the summer." He glanced over her shoulder. "Looks like our students are on the way. Prepare yourself."

"What for?" Elle turned around and had to fight to keep from laughing. The women were all outfitted in typical water-resistant skiwear they'd probably bought in Jackson or in the resort ski shop. The men were a different story. They had the required skis, boots and poles. But they'd dressed for a day riding the range, not a morning on skis. All of them wore jeans, sheepskin jackets, leather gloves and Stetsons.

No, wait. One man was outfitted in ski clothes, a short, barrel-chested guy sporting a handlebar mustache. She'd bet he was the one signed up with the women in Jared's group.

"Good luck," Jared murmured.

"It's only the bunny slope. Shouldn't matter." She counted the men as they approached, and her gaze locked momentarily with Trey's. He grinned, and she couldn't help grinning back. She hoped he felt as great this morning as she did.

But her quick head count gave her seven men instead of six. One of the Last Chance group must have changed his mind and decided to try the sport after all. She wondered if they'd communicated on the dress code or if they'd all come to this Western-wear decision of their own accord.

"Good morning, gentlemen, and welcome." She handed one clipboard to Trey, who'd reached her first, his long strides betraying his eagerness. She gave the other one to the next man, who also wore a mustache, although not of the handlebar variety. "If you'll pass the clipboards around and fill out the required liability form, we can get started. While you're doing that, you can also introduce yourselves."

"I'm Trey Wheeler." He said it as if he'd never met her before. No one smirked or made a comment.

"Gabe Chance," said the man with the sandy mustache.

A green-eyed man next to him spoke up. "Nick Chance."

"We brought him along 'cause he's a veterinarian," Gabe said. "If we break anything, we're covered."

"Good to know, but I'll do my best to make sure that doesn't happen." Elle turned to the next man in the semi-circle.

"Jack Chance."

"Ah. So you decided to join your brothers, after all." Even semi-isolated at the resort, she'd heard of Jack Chance, oldest of the brothers, part Shoshone and acknowledged spokesman for the Chance family in Jackson Hole.

Jack's dark eyes flashed with humor. "I blame tequila shots and my potential ex-buddy Nash Bledsoe here." He glanced over at the cowboy standing next to him. "We have a sizable bet riding on my ability to stick it out this morning."

"I see." This lesson was shaping up to be a memorable one.

"I'm Alex Keller," said a fair-haired man.

"You're the one with some experience," Elle said.

"A little. I'm no expert."

She'd believe that, since he'd chosen to dress in jeans like the rest of them.

"And I'm a total beginner," said a freckle-faced cowboy who looked like the youngest of the group. "Jeb Branford, at your service, ma'am."

"It's great to meet all of you." She smiled at them. "But I have to ask, why the jeans and cowboy hats?"

Alex glanced around the circle. "Told you guys she'd wonder about that."

"We don't own skiing gear," Gabe said. "Seemed kind of silly to buy it for one time."

"True, but you could have rented something."

"That's what Watkins did," the freckle-faced guy named Jeb said. "Mary Lou made him. But the rest of us agreed that those ski pants and puffy jackets look sort of…unmanly." Then he flushed. "I mean, the outfit suits you, ma'am, but we're…we're cowboys."

"Fair enough." Elle bit back a smile. "You should be fine for the bunny slope, but—"

"Damn, is it *really* called the bunny slope?" Jack looked pained.

Nash clapped him on the shoulder. "'Fraid so, Jack, old boy."

"I was hoping that was just you being cute, Nash."

"It is, in fact, the bunny slope," Elle said. "If any of you graduate from the bunny slope, you might want to rethink your outfit. Wet denim can get pretty uncomfortable."

"Which will only be a problem if we fall down," Jack said.

Alex, the one who knew better, smiled. "Good luck with that, Jack."

Jack gazed at him, his expression serenely confident. "Time will tell, won't it? When this is over, we'll compare butts and see who has the dry one."

Elle ducked her head so they couldn't see her expression. If Jack, or any of them, thought they would stay upright throughout this lesson, they were in for quite a surprise. She might have to put on a ski mask so they wouldn't catch her dying of laughter.

"All righty!" She glanced around the group. "After you've signed the form, go on over to the bench and put on your skis. I'm about to put mine on, so if you want to come over and watch how it's done, you're welcome. I'm also sure Alex can help you with that."

Alex nodded. "I remember that much, at least. And something about a pizza wedge and a French fry."

Jeb peered at him. "Are we skiing or eating lunch?"

"Skiing," Alex said. "You'll get it when we start out. I just remember you never want to French fry when you should pizza wedge."

"Very good advice, Alex." Elle wondered if Trey would follow her as she walked over to retrieve her skis. She was grateful when he didn't. She wouldn't mind giving him a private ski lesson, but that would be flaunting their connection, and she didn't want that.

Once her cowboys were lined up with their skis and goggles on, she wished she could take a picture. She doubted Serenity had ever seen anything like it. Amazingly, they had managed to get in line without whacking each other's shins, but it was early yet. "Have any of you gone snowshoeing?" she asked.

Several nodded, including Trey. She filed that away for later. He might not be ready to ski with her by the end of the weekend, but they could take some snowshoes and trek to a private clearing for some quiet time together.

"This isn't like snowshoeing," she said. "Your skis are waxed on the bottom so they slide over the snow, which can be a good thing or a bad thing, depending on whether you're in control."

"That's what we're here to learn," Gabe said.

"It's the most important thing to learn." Elle positioned her goggles on top of her head. "Alex is right about the pizza slice and the French fry position. To slow down, put the tips of your skis together and the tails apart. The larger the pizza slice, the slower you'll go."

They all nodded.

"French fry position means your skis are parallel so you'll go faster. Keep your knees apart at all times. Pretend you're holding a basketball between them."

"Or a flake of hay," Jeb said. "I never played basketball, but I've tossed around plenty of hay."

"A flake of hay, then." Elle got into a basic skiing position. "And keep your knees slightly bent, like I'm doing now, and lean forward a bit. This is not a time to stand tall."

"Can we give it a try?" Nick seemed eager to get started. "The women have started up already."

"So they have." Elle noticed that Jared's group was on the towline headed for the top of the bunny slope. "Any questions before we follow them up there?"

Jeb raised his hand. "What about the falling down part? I know Jack doesn't plan to, but I might."

"Excellent question. If you fall, get your skis parallel to each other and below your body. Also, stay sideways to the hill. Use the slope to push yourself up. I'll be there to help you, so don't worry too much about it. You'll be fine."

"Count on it." Jack led off, and as he did, he called out, "Wagons, ho!"

On cue, the rest started singing the theme song from *Rawhide* as they marched in single file over to the towrope. Elle wished to God she had a video camera. Those cowboys were too cute for words. And one of them, the one she'd had naked in her bed last night, was the cutest of them all.

5

TREY COULDN'T SAY he was the worst skier in the bunch, but he wasn't the best, either. Alex had done this before, so he didn't count, but Jack Chance surprised them all. He took to skiing as if he'd been born with a ski pole in each hand. His jeans stayed dry. Figured. After all, this was Jack they were talking about.

Trey didn't have much natural ability for the sport, apparently, and on top of that, he spent more time watching Elle than practicing his pizza wedge and French fry moves. Clad in black ski pants and jacket, her sleek body was poetry in motion as she swerved among her students, giving tips and helping those who'd fallen.

He and the others, including Alex, had gone down at least once. Trey had landed in the snow twice so far, and both times, just his luck, Alex had come over to help him and make suggestions before Elle could. The third time, though, Elle happened to be closer to him than Alex was. She skied in his direction, moving with grace and efficiency.

About a yard away, she made what he'd learned

was a hockey stop—a quick shift sideways with parallel skis. It created a little spray of snow and looked
impressive. He wanted to learn that, but he needed to
master the pizza wedge first.

"Uncross your skis and scoot around so they're
downhill from you," she said.

His goggles were bugging the hell out of him, so
he shoved them in his jacket pocket. Then he untan-
gled his skis and repositioned his legs downhill of his
body. In the process some snow worked its way under
the hem of his jacket. Damn, that was cold. She'd been
right about wet denim, too. Ski pants were looking
better every second.

Gliding toward him, she swooped down and plucked
his hat out of the snow. "I'm sure you want this."

"I do." He abandoned both poles so he could take it
from her and brush the snow off. "Thanks."

"I have to admit the hats aren't the worst idea in the
world." She pushed her goggles up and gazed at him.
"They stand up to the snow and they shade your eyes."

"Yeah, but we're all losing them like crazy." He put
on his hat and tugged on the brim. "The bunny slope
is littered with Stetsons."

Her laughter made her eyes sparkle. "Next time
you can tie them on."

"Next time I'll wear something else."

"Does that mean you're willing to try this again?"
Still balanced on her skis, she crouched down beside
him.

If he attempted to do that, he would topple over. She
was a superb athlete, and that turned him on. "Sure,
I'll try again. So far I pretty much suck at this, but the
company's great."

"What a nice thing to say."

"Yeah, well, I've been told I'm—" He paused and drew in a sharp breath as the sun emerged from behind a cloud.

"That you're what?"

"It's not important." He gazed at her, entranced by the image that had haunted him for eight months. "You look exactly the way you did when you pulled me out of that snowdrift, except it's the sun making the halo instead of your truck's headlights."

"At least this time you don't have a concussion."

"At least this time I know your name."

"You know a lot more than that about me, cowboy."

He looked into her eyes, and his pulse hammered in response to the desire he saw shining in those blue depths. "And I plan to learn a whole lot more." He was also becoming aroused. His swelling cock pushed painfully against a layer of cold, wet cotton followed by a thicker layer of cold, wet denim. "This isn't the best time to be having this conversation, is it?"

Her mouth curved and she glanced down at his crotch. "Probably not. I can imagine what those wet jeans must feel like."

"They're all that and worse. Any chance you'll come by and help peel them off when this is over?"

"Tempting as that sounds, it's not a good idea." She straightened and pulled her goggles down.

He spoke quickly, wanting to get vital information to her. "Incidentally, your manager, Carl, came looking for me during breakfast in the restaurant."

She lifted the goggles again. "He did?"

"Yeah. Someone told him the story about you rescuing me last spring, and he thought that was kind of cool." Tired of sitting in the snow, he used the slope as leverage and pushed himself upright. He wasn't totally steady, but he was standing. "He wanted to set my mind at ease. He doesn't see a problem with us socializing when you're off duty."

"Socializing." She smiled. "I guess that covers all sorts of things."

"Yes, ma'am, it does."

She held his gaze for a beat. "At the end of the lesson, you should soak in the tub for a while. Your muscles aren't used to this."

"Sounds like you want me to get naked."

Her eyes sparked with mischief. "It's not a bad idea."

"Got any more ideas?"

"I happen to have a two-hour break after this."

That news helped him generate a considerable amount of body heat. "I'm in room 124."

"Okay." Repositioning her goggles, she dug her poles into the snow. "See you then." She sped off to help another fallen cowboy.

He stood there wondering how in hell he was supposed to practice pizza and French fry when his cock was as rigid as a ski pole.

"Trey!"

He recognized Watkins's voice, although he couldn't see the guy. Using his poles to balance himself and wincing at the discomfort in his crotch, he turned cautiously to his right, where Jared's group had been practicing.

So far, the groups hadn't mingled. Trey suspected male pride was involved. The five married guys wanted to perfect their technique before they joined their wives, who had been working with Jared.

Watkins looked pretty damned confident as he stood on the slope in his peacock-blue ski pants and jacket. He'd opted for a matching knit cap, and though Trey could see the sense in that kind of headgear now, it still looked dorky, especially paired with the goggles. Maybe a different color would help.

"Check this out, my friend!" Watkins's grin made his handlebar mustache wiggle. He pushed off, his knees bent as they'd been taught. First he sashayed left, and then he sashayed right, followed by a perfect, snow-spewing hockey stop.

"That's great!" Trey was jealous, but he had no right to be. He'd been lusting after his ski instructor instead of focusing on the task at hand. "Would you be willing to show me how you did that?"

"Absolutely." Watkins used his poles to good effect as he skied toward Trey.

"Wait for me! I'm right behind you!" Mary Lou called out. Sailing over in their direction, she seemed as much at home on her skis as her husband. "Isn't this fun?"

"I'm not sure I'd use that word," Trey said.

Mary Lou looked him up and down. "Of course you wouldn't, dressed like you're heading down to the corral. Why didn't you wear the right stuff?"

"We all thought—"

"Never mind. I had the same argument with Watkins. He couldn't picture himself in ski pants, either."

"But you were right to talk me into it, Lou-Lou. I can move a hundred times better in these." He surveyed Trey's wet jeans. "That denim looks mighty soggy and uncomfortable."

"You have no idea."

"I have some idea. I fell in an icy river once. But maybe you can still learn, even wearing jeans."

"He can," Mary Lou said. "He's young and agile. If old codgers like us can pick it up, so can Trey, despite his wardrobe choices. Come on, son. Show us what you've learned so far."

Trey moved his skis into a good-sized pizza wedge and gradually narrowed it. He began to move slowly down the hill.

"That's it!" Watkins called out. "Good job! Now use your thighs to turn yourself slightly to the left."

"Knees apart!" Mary Lou yelled. "Butt tucked in!"

Trey wished they weren't making so much noise with this instruction, but he had asked them to help, so he'd endure the humiliation. And he actually made a turn.

"Now go the other way!" Being a singer, Watkins knew how to project, so the entire hillside of skiers was probably listening.

"Butt tucked!" Mary Lou wasn't a singer, but she had a good set of vocal cords on her, too.

Trey managed to change course without falling down, while Watkins and Mary Lou cheered. That would have been okay, except that others had joined in, which led Trey to believe he had collected an audience. Not his goal.

But if he had one, he might as well do his best. He executed another turn, and another. At this rate he'd be at the bottom before long.

Behind him, somebody started up a chant—*Wheeler,*

Wheeler, Wheeler. The volume grew as more people joined in. Damn it, this was plain embarrassing. He could fall down at any minute.

In spite of that fear, he was determined to finish with a hockey stop. A fellow couldn't have people chanting his name and then have the performance peter out at the end. Besides, one of those people watching had to be Elle, although he doubted she was chanting. That was more the kind of thing a bunch of cowboys would do to one of their own.

His timing had to be right. One more turn and then the hockey stop. He swerved left, pivoted the way he'd seen Watkins do it, and sent up a decent spray of snow. Cheers erupted as he teetered there for one glorious moment. Then he fell.

The cheers turned into one unison groan. Trey started to chuckle, and the more he thought about that juvenile display of showmanship, the harder he laughed. Good thing he was already on the ground, because doubled over like this, he never would have been able to balance on the damned skis.

Elle got to him first. "Trey! Are you hurt? Can you get up? What's wrong?"

He gulped for air. "I'm fine. Just…laughing my fool head off."

"Oh, good." She sighed in obvious relief. "When I saw you holding your stomach, I thought you'd done something to yourself, although I couldn't imagine what."

Grinning, Trey snapped the catch on his skis and took them off. "That was *almost* impressive."

"I was impressed."

"Glad to hear it. Is this lesson over yet?"

"As a matter of fact, it is. Your timing was perfect, even if your demonstration wasn't. Let me help you up."

"Thanks." He should be embarrassed that a woman was pulling him to his feet, but he'd already made a fool of himself, and he was glad for the support. She'd once hauled him out of a snowdrift, so she certainly had the strength to help him up now.

Besides, this way he got to hold her hand, even if they both had on gloves and he couldn't touch her soft skin. He would be doing that soon, though.

Eventually the rest of the skiers came down the bunny slope, all of them staying on their skis the whole way. They gathered at the spot where Elle and Trey stood. Trey accepted both congratulations and commiserations while they all divested themselves of their skis.

Jared made a megaphone of his hands and got everyone's attention. "I realize everyone will be busy tomorrow with wedding activities, but we can schedule another session the morning after that. How many are in?"

All hands went up, including Trey's.

"I'd advise the cowboys to acquire ski pants," Jared said. "You'll find them a lot more pleasant."

"I'll vouch for that," Watkins said.

"I've got twenty bucks that says Jack won't wear 'em," Nash said.

"You'd lose that bet, my friend," Jack said, "just like you lost the one today."

Nash made a face. "Don't remind me."

"But, Jack, you're the only one who didn't fall

down." Jeb's expression was filled with hero worship. "You don't need to worry about ski pants."

"I didn't fall down, but I'm here to tell you that my boys are *not* happy." Jack glanced around at his jeans-wearing companions. "The next time I come out here, my guys will be thermally protected and water-proofed. Count on it."

After the laughter died down, the crowd dispersed with much joking about frosty denim and shrinkage. Trey would have liked to confirm with Elle that they'd meet in his room when she was free, but she was having a long conversation with Jared. Trey decided to go back to his room and get free of the cursed jeans.

Watkins called out as Trey started toward the lodge. The barrel-chested cowboy had his cell phone in his hand.

Trey paused. "What's up?"

"I have a call from Pam." He put the phone to his ear and continued to talk as he approached. "Let me check with him, Pam. Should be fine." He put his thumb over the speaker and glanced at Trey. "As we might expect, Emmett's freaking out a little about all the fuss surrounding the ceremony."

"What fuss?"

"You and I haven't been part of it, but Pam's been in consultation with the chef about the menu because some items didn't come in as expected, and the florist shipped the wrong arrangements and Emmett's coat doesn't fit quite right. You know, the usual wedding issues."

"If you say so. I've only been involved in one wedding, and that was when Sarah and Pete got married last August. I'm not what you'd call an experienced wedding person."

"The upshot is, Emmett is stressed. Pam thinks it'll help if we meet in the room where the ceremony will be held and give them a little preview of the music we intend to play. She thinks just listening to those songs he loves, songs he helped choose, will remind him of how great the wedding is going to be."

"I'm not sure that will work. It might make him more nervous than ever."

Watkins nodded. "It could, but she's running out of ideas short of plying him with whiskey."

"Isn't there a bachelor party for him tonight? We can get him toasted then."

"And we will, but it's quite a few hours between now and the bachelor party. Anyway, I think we should give it a shot."

"You bet. After all, she's rolled out the red carpet for all of us. Does she want us to do the preview now?"

"Yep. As soon as we can change out of our ski duds, or in your case, out of your wet jeans."

"Oh."

"You got something planned?"

"Not exactly, but…" Trey couldn't very well explain to Watkins what he'd scheduled for the next couple of hours.

"Something to do with our ski instructor, maybe?"

Trey's face grew hot.

"Look, ordinarily I'd put Pam off for a little while, but she sounded desperate. If you want me to go down there and handle it by myself, I will."

As a testament to his driving need for Elle, Trey considered that offer, but only for a split second. "No, that wouldn't be right. I'll go. Give me fifteen minutes to change clothes and grab my guitar. I'll meet you in the lobby."

"Thanks." Watkins squeezed his shoulder. "I know Pam is going to really appreciate this."

"I'm sure she will." Trey glanced back at Elle, who was still talking to Jared. How could he let her know the plan had changed?

Too bad he didn't have her cell number. He'd get it first chance he had, but for now he'd have to stop by her room and slip a note under her door. That wasn't great, but it was the best he could come up with on short notice.

Knowing he needed time to write and deliver the note before he met Watkins in the lobby, he made tracks for his room, which fortunately was on the first floor. He took off his gloves and jacket on the way there. That soak in the tub wouldn't be happening.

Inside his room, he tossed his coat on a chair and pulled off his clothes as fast as his cold fingers allowed. Then he grabbed a towel from the bathroom and rubbed it briskly over his chilled body. Ah, better. Not as good as a soak in the tub, and definitely not as good as making love to Elle, but he'd survive.

As he finished his rubdown, he heard a knock at the door. He wrapped the towel around his waist and checked the peephole. Maybe Pam had changed her mind and Watkins had come down to tell him. He could only hope.

Instead, he discovered Elle, still in her ski clothes, outside his door. He pulled it open. "I—"

"Don't talk." She hurried inside and began tearing off her jacket. "I have five minutes. Jared's driving into town to look at some new ski equipment for the lodge and needs me to go. The sale ends today. I couldn't get out of it." She dropped the jacket and knelt down to take off her boots.

"But you still want to—"

"Oh, yeah." She glanced up, and her blue gaze was full of fire as she dispensed with her boots. "I want to."

He dropped the towel.

6

Elle had known the sensible thing to do—cancel having sex with Trey. On her way to his room, she'd conducted an inner debate. Her sensible self had put up a really good argument about not appearing too eager.

Except she was eager, and not totally rational, either. A rational woman would have called his room to say she couldn't make it. The devil in her had whispered that it would be quicker to simply stop by.

Once she'd decided on that course of action, she'd begun to consider another one. Finding him wrapped in a towel had been the deciding factor. Seeing how quickly he reacted to her suggestion had told her she'd made the right choice.

She stood and shoved her ski pants and silk long johns to the floor. He, however, hadn't moved, except for the elegant rise of his cock. "You'd better get the—"

"Right." He spun away from her and headed for the closet.

She noticed a tattoo on his left biceps as he turned away. She didn't get a clear look, but thought it might be a wing of some kind. Now was not the time to ask about it, though.

She pulled her turtleneck over her head and dropped it on the pile of clothes at her feet. Crossing to his king-size bed, she threw back the covers, scattering decorative pillows everywhere. By the time she'd climbed in one side, he'd climbed in the other.

They met in the middle, his mouth hungrily seeking hers as he moved between her thighs. One quick thrust and he was there, right where she ached to have him. The pressure set off tiny explosions that reverberated through her.

His mouth lifted, hovering over hers. "Promise we'll have longer tonight."

Breathless with need and not caring that he knew, she pressed her fingers into his back. "I promise. But I need you now."

"I need you, too." He began to pump, first slowly and then faster. "So...oh, God...so much." His breathing grew ragged as he pounded into her with enough force to lift her from the bed.

She rode the whirlwind with him, arching her back and urging him on. "Yes, oh, *yes*. Keep doing that. Right there...right..." She came in a fiery rush, and he swiftly followed her into the flames with a deep groan of surrender.

She gulped for air. "So good."

"Yeah." He kissed her once, hard. "Tonight," he murmured as he levered himself away from her.

"Yes." Quivering in the aftermath of her orgasm, she forced herself to slide out of his bed. He'd already disappeared into the bathroom.

She'd loved every minute of that experience, but

she'd love every minute of a longer one, too. Jared's request faded in importance. "Should I text Jared and beg off?"

"No." He walked out of the bathroom, a study in masculine beauty.

"Are you sure?" She admired his chest, furred with dark hair, and followed the line of hair to his navel and beyond, where dark curls framed his semierect cock and impressive balls. Her body grew moist and achy all over again.

"I'm sure. I can't stay, either. Pam Mulholland asked Watkins and me to give her a preview of the wedding music."

"Now?"

"Yep. I'm meeting Watkins in the lobby. He may already be there."

"Whoops. We'd better get moving, then." As she stooped to gather her clothes, the humor of the situation made her smile. "You could have given me a rain check, you know."

"Are you kidding?" He opened a drawer and got out a pair of briefs.

"No." She dressed quickly. She'd rather not be here if Watkins got tired of waiting and came looking for Trey. "I would have understood."

"Lady, I'm no fool. Opening my door to find you ready and willing was a gift. I wasn't about to say no to an opportunity like that." He grabbed jeans and a shirt and put them on as he talked. "I'll be smiling all day."

"Better be careful. People will wonder what you've been up to."

"Are you worried about that?" He sat on the bed

and pulled on his boots. "What people think of us getting together?"

"I'm not super worried, but I'm not used to having everyone know my business." She hadn't realized that was a priority with her until now, but maybe that was a big reason why she'd always kept her personal life separated from work. Not dating resort guests, both here and in Argentina, had guaranteed her privacy.

"Then we'll keep it on the down-low." He stood and picked up his guitar case. "Ready?"

"Yes." She zipped her jacket. "If you're going toward the lobby, I'll go in the opposite direction."

"Before we leave, give me your cell number, in case you get some free time this afternoon."

She grabbed a pad and pen from his desk and scribbled it down. "I doubt it. Jared and I are scheduled to make a promo video for the resort's ski program. But just in case, let me have yours, too."

He tore off the bottom of the page she handed him, wrote his number and gave it to her. "And I need one more kiss."

"Make it a quickie."

He laughed. "I think we already did that." Setting down his guitar, he drew her into his arms. His kiss wasn't quick at all. He lingered and tasted, teased and nibbled.

She moaned softly and drew back. "No fair. You've stirred me up again."

"Just making sure you'll show up here tonight after the bachelor party."

"We'll meet in your room, then?"

"My bed's bigger."

"Good point."

A sharp rap on the door made them jump apart.

Trey mouthed the name *Watkins*.

"I'll hide in the bathroom and leave after you do," she murmured.

He nodded and picked up his guitar.

She put a restraining hand on his arm, stood on tiptoe and finger-combed his tousled hair into place. Now he didn't look quite as much like a man who'd been rolling around in bed with a woman. Then she retreated to the bathroom and listened as Trey apologized to Watkins for being late.

"Hey, no worries," Watkins said. "When you didn't show up in the lobby, I wondered if we had our wires crossed. Is everything okay?"

"Everything is great. Just had to warm up a little is all," Trey said as he closed the door behind him.

They'd been gone only a couple of seconds when Elle's phone, which she'd tucked in the pocket of her jacket, chimed. No surprise—it was Jared—but she was grateful he hadn't called a minute ago. She answered it with a cheery greeting.

Jared sounded slightly impatient. "I thought I'd hear from you by now."

"Sorry. Something came up." *Did it ever.* "I'll be down in the lobby in ten minutes." She'd have to race back to her room like an Olympian and freshen up in record time, but she could do it.

"Okay. See you then. Hurry. This kind of sale doesn't come around often. Carl's eager to cash in on it, and he wants you to check out the snowboards, since you've had more experience with them than I have."

Elle understood the urgency. The resort got a volume discount from this store, and a sale on top of that could save significant money. Usually she enjoyed shopping for winter sports equipment.

But as she flew back to her room and shucked her clothes for the second time, her thoughts were on the glories of making love to Trey. She expected that once the newness wore off, she wouldn't be so focused on him.

Their relationship was really only about sex, and that would get old eventually. It always had before with other guys. Elle wasn't even sure that she and Trey would have things to talk about if they weren't locked together in feverish delight.

He was a cowboy and she was a ski instructor, so their career paths had nothing in common. She had no knowledge of horses and all he knew about skiing he'd picked up this morning. She was well traveled thanks to her parents' military lifestyle and her own decision to spend six months on each side of the equator. Trey might be a globe-trotter, but she doubted it.

Frankly, she didn't care if he shared her love of travel and skiing. She wasn't looking for a lifetime companion and she'd made that clear. At least she hoped he wouldn't misunderstand her sexual eagerness for something deeper and more meaningful.

Maybe she needed to reemphasize her philosophy tonight. The sex was terrific, and she'd love to partake as often as possible while he was here, but that didn't mean she was falling for him. She'd look for any signs that he had a different idea about how things were working out between them.

If he did hope for more than sex from her, she'd have to break it off. Selfishly, she didn't want to do that. Sex had never been this good before. But she couldn't continue to indulge if she thought Trey would end up with a broken heart.

Emmett was already in the room that had been designated for the wedding ceremony when Trey and Watkins arrived. Pam was nowhere to be seen, though. The decorating had begun, although no one besides Emmett was in the room now.

Trey thought it was a fine spot for a wedding—not too big and not too small. He estimated that about sixty folding chairs had been set up, with an aisle down the middle. Pine boughs were everywhere—over the arched windows and covering a trellis that would serve as the focal point for the ceremony.

Wine-colored ribbons were woven among the boughs, and the same color was used for cushions on the dark wood folding chairs and the runner down the middle of the aisle. The room looked classy and smelled wonderful, and Trey figured the staff wasn't even finished.

Emmett didn't seem to be enjoying the ambiance, though, as he paced in the back of the room. In his sixties, Emmett looked like the quintessential ranch foreman with his tall, lanky physique, clear blue eyes and carefully trimmed gray mustache. He was completely at home on the back of a horse or pitching hay into a stall, but he appeared ill at ease in a room filled with expensive wood paneling, thick carpeting and crystal chandeliers.

He spotted them and walked over immediately. "I'm glad you boys are here. I have this great idea, but I can't get Pam on board with it. I'm hoping you two can help me convince her."

Watkins set down his guitar case, and Trey followed suit. "What idea is that?" Watkins asked.

Emmett rubbed his hands together, betraying his nervousness. "Pam and I can fly to Vegas this afternoon, get married tonight, and fly back here tomorrow. Then we can all party, just like she planned."

Watkins stared at him. "Emmett, that's not going to work."

"No, it isn't," Trey added. "I'm the new guy, so I don't know all the history, but I can't see that happening."

"Why not?" Emmett's jaw tightened. "The main thing is the party, right?"

"Uh, no," Watkins said. "The main thing is folks witnessing the ceremony when you and Pam get hitched. They're all looking forward to that."

"I don't know why they want to sit through some boring ceremony." Emmett caught himself. "I don't mean to say your music will be boring, you understand. That will be first-rate. But you'll still play for the party when everyone can dance instead of being stuck in these rows of chairs."

"Watkins is right," Trey said. "They're looking forward to the ceremony itself. You and Pam are important to them, and they want to be part of this wedding. I don't think it'll work for you to fly off to Vegas."

"And I doubt Pam would go, anyway," Watkins added. "You can't get married in Vegas without a bride."

"See, that's where you two come in." Emmett began to pace again, waving his arms as he walked. "If you both tell her it's a great idea, she might listen. I've tried to get Emily on board, but my stubborn daughter won't hear of it. I've talked to Sarah and that didn't go well, either." He turned to Watkins. "I even tried talking to Mary Lou a few minutes ago. She popped in to see how the decorations were coming along. She's completely against the Vegas plan."

"That doesn't surprise me," Watkins said.

"It surprised me! You and Mary Lou got married on a damned Panama Canal cruise, for God's sake! You didn't go through all this foolishness!"

"You're right about the cruise." In a gesture that said Watkins was stalling for time so he could think, he took off his hat, still damp from the snow, and brushed a speck of lint from the crown. Then he repositioned the hat on his head and glanced up at Emmett. "I'm Mary Lou's husband, so I understand where you're coming from."

"I knew you would. You need to get me out of this circus. The party's okay. I'm fine with the party. It's standing up in front of a room full of people dressed in a coat that doesn't fit right, and saying those words, which should be private, in front of all those folks…"

"You and Mary Lou are alike in that. She didn't want a big deal, either, especially because we'd both been dodging the question of marriage for so many years."

"Exactly! Just like Pam and me. So why won't Mary Lou back me on this? She of all people should understand."

Watkins shook his head. "When you put it like that, I'm not sure I have the answer."

"Look," Trey said. "You can disregard me if you want, but maybe it's because Mary Lou can see it from a different angle this time."

Watkins turned to gaze at him. "That's smart thinking, son. Plus we just had Sarah and Pete's wedding in August, which everybody, including Mary Lou, enjoyed so much. She might understand a little better now why it's important to let folks be a part of a wedding ceremony."

Emmett sighed. "You're saying I have to take one for the team, aren't you?"

"Well, and for Pam," Watkins said. "You love her, right?"

"I've loved her for years."

"There you go." Watkins smiled. "If saying her vows in front of all her friends and family will make her happy, then you gotta do it."

Emmett scrubbed a hand over his face and looked at them. "Guess so."

As if on cue, Pam walked into the room. "There you two are! Ready to play for us?" She was dressed in a cheerful red velour sweat suit, and not a blond hair was out of place in her chin-length bob, but her bright tone sounded forced.

"You know what?" Emmett walked over and put his arms around her. "We don't need a preview."

Her body stiffened. "Why not?"

"These boys will do a fine job. I don't think we need to worry about their performance. This wedding's going to be great."

Pam looked stunned. "It is?"

"Yep. I can hardly wait." He glanced over at Trey and Watkins. "See you both at the bachelor party tonight. In the meantime, I'm going to have a long and very private lunch with my fiancée."

"See you tonight!" Watkins picked up his guitar case and motioned to Trey. "Let's go, cowboy."

Trey grabbed his guitar and followed Watkins out of the room, but he couldn't resist glancing back at Emmett and Pam. Pam looked as if someone had just handed her the moon.

Her expression haunted Trey as he said goodbye to Watkins and walked back to his room. The covers on the bed and the scattered pillows bore mute testimony to the wild passion that he'd shared with Elle less than an hour ago. But it wasn't love that she felt for him.

If he was honest with himself, he'd have to say that no woman had ever looked at him the way Pam had looked at Emmett. They'd desired him, but they hadn't gazed at him with their heart in their eyes.

He'd imagined himself in love several times, but had he been? Or had he been in love with the idea of love? If so, then he needed to grow up. This emotion he felt for Elle seemed substantial, but he couldn't swear it was love. It could be gratitude mixed with her mystery-woman allure and his intense sexual attraction to her.

Watkins had known Mary Lou for years. Emmett had known Pam for years. Trey had known Elle for less than twenty-four hours. During that time they'd had some amazing sex, but not much conversation.

If he expected Elle to ever look at him the way Pam had looked at Emmett, then he needed to spend time getting to know her and letting her get to know him. That probably meant—and this was a slightly depressing conclusion—not having sex.

Or maybe they could have sex, because they both wanted to, and then they could have a long conversation. He wasn't even sure she'd be interested in having a long conversation with him. Maybe all she cared about was the sex. That thought was the most depressing of all.

If it was true, though, he might as well find out now. He'd started out wanting Elle in his bed, which was a goal any man with a pulse would understand. She was just that hot. But now he wanted more than that for the two of them.

Maybe he'd subconsciously had that goal all along, but until seeing Pam and Emmett together, he hadn't realized how much he wanted their kind of relationship. He didn't want to wait years for it, either.

7

THE SHOPPING TRIP to Jackson took much longer than Elle would have liked, but Jared seemed in no hurry. All thoughts of squeezing in an hour of alone time with Trey disappeared. Once they returned to the resort, making the video sapped the rest of the day.

By the time Elle glanced at her watch, it was time for the bachelor party to begin in the bar. Fred was working the party, giving Amy the night off, which meant Elle wouldn't be asked to help out. That gave her no choice but to wait for Trey's call signaling the end of the bachelor party.

She decided to use the time to decorate her Christmas tree, but the tree was small and her decorations few. She liked Christmas well enough, but having two parents in the military had meant that anything could come up to derail the holidays—a move or a deployment of one parent or the other. Her mother and father had never established family traditions. Flexibility had been the key element for the Mastersons, and Elle had grown up thinking traditions weren't necessary to a happy life.

That made her the perfect employee for a resort that offered Christmas holiday ski packages. She worked straight through, which allowed both Jared and Annalise to spend a few days at home with their extended families. Her parents treated Christmas so casually that it seemed silly for her to fly thousands of miles to be with them for the holidays.

She hung the last ornament on her tree long before she could expect Trey to call or text, so she decided to turn on her computer and do a Google search for the Last Chance Ranch. Now that she'd met all three Chance brothers, she was curious about the place. She vaguely remembered that they sold horses, so they should have a website.

Wow, did they ever have a website! The images were spectacular, and she quickly realized why. Dominique Chance, Nick's wife and one of the skiers this morning, was a professional photographer. Elle had seen her work in the windows of a gallery in Jackson. Naturally Dominique would make sure the ranch and its paint horses were shown off to good advantage.

Elle lost herself in exploring the site, all the while picturing Trey there. She read the history of the place—how Archibald Chance had won it in a poker game during the Great Depression of the 1930s. The centerpiece of the ranch, a mammoth two-story log house with wings extending at an angle on each side, looked like something out of a movie.

During the summer months, the ranch house opened its doors to disadvantaged boys, eight per season. They lived and worked on the ranch from the middle of June to the middle of August. An application form was available on the site.

Elle found it significant that the charitable program was as prominent on the home page as the paints that were the ranch's bread and butter. She didn't know much about horses, but she could appreciate the beauty of the ones in the photos. One arresting image showed Jack Chance dressed all in black and mounted on a black-and-white stallion named Bandit.

No doubt about it, there was something very sexy about a square-jawed cowboy sitting on a powerful horse. She mentally substituted Trey for Jack in the picture. Yum. She could picture him racing across a grassy meadow, leaning over the horse's neck, his body in tune with the fluid motion of the horse.

She wouldn't ever see that, of course. She'd be in Argentina during the months that Trey could conceivably be riding the range doing his cowboy thing. They'd be thousands of miles apart, their short fling forgotten.

Maybe he'd find a cowgirl at that bar Jared had mentioned in the little town of Shoshone, near the ranch. She couldn't remember the name of the bar, so she typed *Shoshone* into Google and found it. The Spirits and Spurs was owned by Jack's wife, Josie, who'd also been on the bunny slope today. The bar, more than a hundred years old, got its name from the ghosts who haunted the place—miners and cowhands who'd bought drinks there for generations.

Even though she kept reminding herself that she would never set foot in the bar, she was intrigued. It also provided live music every night during the summer, another feature she wouldn't be able to enjoy. Trey probably played there, at least once in a while. She was sure that whenever he performed, he would attract the attention of both local girls and tourists passing through.

Did that knowledge bother her and make her jealous? Hell, yes. She had absolutely no right to be jealous of whoever caught his fancy, but the thought of Trey getting jiggy with another woman was decidedly unpleasant.

She'd have to work on that reaction. She couldn't very well plan to have a casual fling with the man and then expect him to be celibate for the rest of his life because he'd be spoiled for anyone else. Unfortunately, she was a little worried that she might be spoiled for anyone else after the incredible sex they'd had and promised to have again.

As if thinking about that activity prompted it, her cell phone pinged with an incoming text. She grabbed her phone eagerly. Winding down. Should be about 10 min. Will text when on my way.

Heat swirled through her. She thought she'd been calmly waiting for this text, but apparently not. The phone shook in her hand as she tried to reply with a simple OK, see you soon. She took a deep breath and managed to punch the right letters.

Now what? She had the sudden urge to take a quick shower. And shave her legs. She accomplished that in record time. As she dried off and lotioned up, she thought about what to wear. Nothing too revealing and sexy. Although that would be fun, she'd be walking the halls, where she might meet people.

But she certainly didn't have to put on underwear. Finally, she settled on jade-green yoga pants and a matching sweatshirt. Easy on, easy off. She got hot again thinking about that. She had some slip-on running shoes without backs. Those would do for her feet.

She put on a little makeup because, once again, she'd be walking the halls and could run into people who might wonder why she looked ready for bed. Ah, she was *so* ready for bed. Brushing her hair, she left it loose.

Her phone pinged again, and adrenaline rushed through her system a second time. She picked it up. On my way.

Heart racing, she texted him back. Me too. Pocketing her room key and her phone, in case she needed to set an alarm, she turned off all the lights and left her room. She didn't want someone to see a light in her window at three in the morning and ask her about it.

As she took the stairs to the first floor and walked through the double doors into the guest portion of the hallway, she saw a cluster of guys talking and laughing near one of the suites. They behaved in the jovial way of men who were slightly drunk. She thought she recognized the Chance brothers, who were with an older man she hadn't met.

They'd probably all attended the bachelor party. She hadn't thought about it until now, but Trey might be under the influence, too. Liquor usually flowed freely at such events. Could be an interesting evening.

The four men in the hallway were busy joking with one another. Although she'd have to walk past them, they might be too involved to notice her. She could only hope.

As she drew closer, she confirmed that the three younger men were the Chance brothers. The older guy had a handmade card stuck in his hatband that said Groom. Must be Emmett Sterling.

"Give me one good reason why I can't sleep with my fiancée tonight," he said in a voice that carried down the hall. Yes, he was definitely tipsy.

Nick Chance stuck one finger in the air and belted out, "Tradition!"

"It ain't mine," Emmett said with a grin. "So back off, boys. I'm goin' in."

"I'd advise against it." Gabe put a restraining hand on his shoulder. "You've slipped your little love note under the door, so we need to get goin'. I'm sure she told you about this program, buddy. She's a thorough lady, and she would've mentioned it."

"Yeah, but she was only joshin'."

Gabe glanced over at Nick. "You think she was kidding, bro?"

Nick shook his head. "Not when I talked to her. She wanted to be *A-L-O-N-E* tonight."

"Oh, she just thinks she does. I'll convince her different," Emmett said.

Head down to hide a smile, Elle walked faster. Maybe she could scoot past while they were arguing this delicate point.

"Emmett, this is why Pam got you a different room for tonight." Jack sounded reasonable and patient. "She wouldn't do that if she didn't mean it."

"But I still got a key for *this* one, and I know how to use it. I'll surprise her. She loves surprises."

Unable to help herself, Elle snuck a peek at the action. Emmett fished a card key from his pocket and started for the door. Feisty guy.

"Hang on, there, cowboy." Nick caught his arm.

"Sorry, Emmett." Jack plucked the key from his hand. "If we let you go through that door, our ass is grass. We promised Pam. The elevator's right down this way." With a glance at Nick, he took Emmett's other arm. "What d'ya say we mosey in that direction, just for fun?"

"Fun means moseying through that door. Bunch of spoilsports." But Emmett allowed himself to be turned.

That put all four of them on a collision course with Elle. She'd been too busy eavesdropping and hadn't moved fast enough. She smiled brightly, pretending that she had not been listening in on their exchange. "Hi there, gentlemen! Did you have a good time at the bachelor party?"

"We surely did." Jack turned to Emmett. "Emmett Sterling, our esteemed groom, I'd like you to meet our equally esteemed ski instructor, Elle Masterson."

"Nice to meet you, ma'am." Emmett touched the brim of his hat. "Thought about getting out there on the bunny slope, but Pam and I decided I might break something, which would mess up our honeymoon."

"I understand."

"Say, what's this I hear about you being the young lady who pulled Trey Wheeler out of a snowdrift last spring?"

Hearing Trey's name mentioned when she was on her way to have sex with the guy made her blush. "Fortunately I came along right after he flipped his Jeep."

Emmett nodded. "I'm mighty glad you did. He's a good hand and plays that guitar of his real nice, too. Kept us plenty entertained tonight."

"I'm glad." Dear God, how she wished that her

blush would fade, but Trey was a subject guaranteed to put pink in her cheeks.

"I assume you're free tomorrow afternoon and evening," Emmett said, "since we're your only responsibility and we sure as hell won't be out skiing then."

Carl had given her the day off, which wouldn't help her at all when it came to Trey, who would be at the wedding. "I thought I'd do a little skiing on my own," she said.

"Ah, you can do that anytime." Emmett waved a dismissive hand. "Come to the wedding and watch me get hitched. Ceremony's at two, but you'd best get there early and grab a good seat."

"Thank you so much, but I don't want to intrude." That much was true, but she wouldn't mind getting to hear Trey and Watkins perform.

"Emmett wouldn't ask if he didn't mean it," Jack said. "It's a great idea. We're all grateful for what you did for Trey. You'd be most welcome."

"Absolutely," Nick added. "You have to come. I'm sure Pam would want you there, too."

Gabe grinned at her. "It'll be the wedding of the century. You don't want to miss that, do you?"

She laughed. "Not when you put it that way. Thank you. I'll be there."

"Good. That's settled." Emmett looked pleased. "Now, before you go, I have an important question to ask. Normally I wouldn't discuss this in public, but I've had a few drinks, so my tongue's loosened up a bit. And you're a woman."

"Yes, I am. Excellent observation."

"A mighty pretty woman, at that. Anyway, as a

woman, what do you think of keeping a man and his fiancée apart the night before they get hitched?"

Elle glanced at Jack, whose eyebrows rose expressively. She understood his silent request that she help the cause, not hinder it.

As it happened, she was glad to. "I think it's sweet," she said, earning her a big smile from Jack. "Old-fashioned, maybe, but sweet. It gives you a chance to miss each other a little, and that will make the wedding night even better."

"Hmm." Emmett stroked his mustache. "Hadn't thought of that. Might be true. Guess I'm okay with it."

"If that's settled, we'd best be off," Nick said. "Big day tomorrow."

"Yep." Elle was more than ready to be on her way, too.

The men all said their good-nights and touched the brims of their hats in farewell.

"Thanks again for the invitation," Elle said.

"We'll be expecting you." Jack met her gaze. "Have a good night, Elle."

"Thanks." She'd probably imagined a gleam of mischief in Jack's dark eyes. As she continued down the hall, she told herself he didn't know where she was going. Yeah, right. Why else would she be roaming the halls at one in the morning if not to pay a call on the cowboy in room 124—the very cowboy they'd just been discussing?

AFTER ELLE'S EAGERNESS that morning, Trey halfway expected her to beat him to the room. Instead, he had time to straighten the covers on the bed and retrieve a couple of condoms from his duffel bag. He'd bought more in one of the resort shops devoted to toiletries and over-the-counter medicine.

When she still hadn't arrived, he sat on the bed and took off his boots. Then he stripped his belt from its loops and laid that on the dresser. After that, he had to stop himself from taking off everything else. Not cool. She might have caught him wearing only a towel this morning, but his showing up at the door like that again would lack class.

Yet he was too agitated to sit still. Laughing to himself, he thought of his original plan to have an in-depth conversation with Elle before getting naked. Good thing he'd shelved that idea. But he hadn't given up on the concept of getting to know her better, and vice versa.

Their current situation put a premium on having sex, because they didn't have the luxury of time. Maybe, after the wedding was over, they'd have that luxury. She'd still be working, though. He had a lot more questions than answers right now.

High on the list was wondering where the hell she was. He'd made the trip from his room to hers, even gotten lost, and it hadn't taken him this long. He glanced at his phone, both to check the time and see if she'd texted. Okay, she wasn't *that* late. His perception of time was skewed by his impatience.

At long last, the knock came. He hurried over and stubbed his toe on the desk chair. Swearing under his breath, he threw open the door.

"I got held up."

"Never mind that." He pulled her into the room, kicked the door shut and filled his arms full of warm, fragrant Elle. "God, you feel good." He rained kisses on her upturned face. "And smell good." He delved into her mouth. "And taste good," he murmured, lifting his head and changing the angle so he could go deeper.

Nudging off her shoes, she pressed her sweet body against his, and unless he was mistaken, she didn't have anything on under her yoga pants. He slid both hands inside her waistband and encountered her bare, sexy bottom. Not even a thong presented a barrier to his questing fingers.

His lips hovered over hers. "I like this decision."

"I wish you'd shown up in a towel."

"Didn't want to be repetitive and boring." He pushed the yoga pants down her hips and kneaded her sleek little derriere.

"Trust me, not boring."

"I'll keep that in mind." He reached between her thighs. "You're soaking wet."

She moaned softly. "Your fault."

"And I could drive nails with my cock."

Her laughter was breathless. "Maybe…" She gulped as he caressed her. "Maybe we should do something about that."

"Good idea." Cupping her bottom, he lifted her up. Her yoga pants fell to the floor as he cradled her against his jutting fly.

"Excellent move." She wrapped her legs around him.

He carried her the short distance to the bed and lowered her to the mattress. Then he followed her down and wedged his aching cock, trapped behind his fly, between her thighs.

She squeezed her legs tighter, and her voice was

ragged. "I'll bet…if you stayed right there…I could come."

"Want to?" He rocked his hips forward, pressing against her heat as he nibbled on her mouth.

She sucked in a breath. "I like the old-fashioned way."

"Then turn me loose. I'll take off my—"

"Can't wait that long." She relaxed her thighs and reached for the button below his navel. "Need you now."

Lust scorched a path straight to his groin. "Go for it." While she dealt with his zipper, he grabbed a condom on the bedside table. But when she pushed down his briefs and got both her hands on him, he groaned and nearly dropped the packet on the floor.

Desperation made him hold on to it. He ripped it open with his teeth, and she took over from there. He was breathing like a charging bull by the time she finished rolling it on, and then he was afraid he acted like one, too.

One of these times he would use more finesse when he engaged in this activity with her, but now wasn't that time. Now was about thrusting home with no hesitation or apology. Fortunately, she didn't seem to mind at all.

In fact, she seemed very pleased with his randy behavior, judging from the way she urged him on. She used some pretty earthy language to do it, too, and he loved that. She was no shy maid, his Elle.

Maybe he didn't know a lot of things about her, but he knew how she responded to sexual pleasure. She gave it everything she had, which inspired him to do the same. He didn't need to think about holding back and waiting for her orgasm, because she let him know it was right around the bend.

He could go headlong and seek the climax he craved. He could ride her with fierce energy because she asked him to. Hell, she begged him to. He could use the same four-letter words she used to describe the hot sex they were sharing.

She was, hands down, the best partner he'd ever had. Yeah, they'd have a conversation eventually, but he believed they were having one now. And this one counted, too. Oh, yeah, it counted.

She cried out and arched under him mere seconds before he came in a glorious rush that made him dizzy. They clung to each other and gasped for breath in unison. He didn't know what else they'd find in common, what other pleasures they'd share, but this…this was unbelievable. And so right.

8

"THAT WAS PLAIN FUN." Elle gazed up at Trey. It had taken them a while, but they were finally breathing normally again.

"Can't say I've ever had more fun in my life." Levering himself up on his forearms, he glanced down at her green velour jacket, which had remained zipped throughout. "But you must be ready to get rid of extra wardrobe items. I sure am."

"I suppose. I got a little sweaty under this thing, but the immediacy of it all was darned exciting." That was putting it mildly. She'd never done it when the guy had his pants on, or mostly on. "Thanks for indulging me."

"My pleasure. Literally. It turns me on that you couldn't wait. I also like that you got so graphic." His cock, still firm and tucked securely within her, twitched. "I'm still liking it, in fact. Keep talking."

She laughed. "It's a function of the moment. I don't normally use that kind of language."

"I figured not."

"So I didn't shock you?"

"Nope."

"You…you make me want to say those things."

"I do? Don't get me wrong. I love that you feel so uninhibited with me, but why?"

She had to think about that. "Maybe because our connection is so basic. And maybe because we didn't find out a lot about each other before we had sex."

"Huh."

"If I'd known more about your background, I would have wondered if I should use those words. Am I making any sense?"

An emotion flickered in his dark eyes. "Guess so. You're saying that we're all about the sex. No complications."

Well, yes, she was saying that, but she wished he looked a little happier about it. Because they craved each other with such intensity, she'd begun to believe this hot, temporary fling was working for both of them. "Is that a problem for you?"

His expression lightened immediately. "Hell, no. Only a fool would have a problem with incredible sex." Breaking eye contact, he drew down the zipper on her sweatshirt. "And the night is young."

"Technically, it's not." The cool air felt lovely on her overheated breasts. Under his gaze, her nipples tightened.

"I know, but we're just getting started." He grazed the tip of each nipple with his palm, and that whisper of a connection made her womb throb.

He glanced up. His voice was low and rough with awareness. "I felt that."

"I can't help it. When you touch me, I…" She moaned as he spread his fingers over her moist skin and pressed gently. A spasm shook her.

"Stay here."

"Oh, don't worry. I will." She couldn't move if the place caught on fire. She was too turned on.

Easing away from her, he left the bed. In moments he was back, and the lamplight gleamed on his naked body, which was as sweaty as hers. "This time, by God, we're going to take it slow."

She gazed at his erect cock and smiled. "You sure about that, cowboy?"

"I'm positive about that, lady. For starters, I want you to sit up, scoot back a ways and take your jacket off."

"Sounds as if you have a plan."

"I do."

Her body hummed with anticipation as she followed his instructions. She wondered if he'd called her *lady* on purpose, echoing her use of *cowboy*. Labels weren't as intimate as first names. Maybe he was going to be okay with keeping this arrangement casual, after all.

"Spread your legs."

"This is getting more interesting by the second."

"That's the idea." Throwing back the covers, he climbed in. He sat facing her, his legs apart, too. "Come a little closer. Prop your thighs on mine."

"Have you been reading *The Kama Sutra?*"

"I paged through it once in the library. Come a few inches forward so we can reach each other. I want you within kissing distance."

As she adjusted her position, she held on to his muscled arms for balance. She glanced at the tattoo. Maybe she wouldn't ask him, after all. Personal details were best left unexplained if she wanted to maintain a no-strings liaison with him.

"Perfect." Cupping her face, he leaned in for a kiss.

She decided to cup something a little lower. She might be within kissing distance, but that put him within fondling distance. She took a notion to make use of her close proximity to his family jewels.

Leaning back, he grasped her wrists and lifted her hands to his shoulders. "Not yet."

"What, there are rules to this game?"

"Yeah, kind of. Let's see how long we can stay like this, touching each other, caressing each other, but not coming."

"So the winner is the last one to cross the finish line?"

"That's right. If you hold off as long as you can, it's supposed to make your climax a whole lot more powerful."

She laughed. "More powerful than I've already had with you? Are you trying to kill me?"

"I'm trying to make this last a while. Each time we've gotten together, we've been so frantic for each other that we've gone straight for the easy climax. Let's slow it down a little. Play around. Get creative."

"Exactly. That's what I was trying to do."

"But we need to start at the top and work our way down. If you start *there,* we'll be done before you know it."

"Oh. Okay. I'm down with that." She gazed at him and realized that she'd never slid her fingers through his dark hair. Its wavy thickness invited a woman's touch.

He wore his hair on the longish side, although not quite collar-length. The style fit his musician persona.

Other than grabbing his head in a fit of passion, she hadn't spent much time fooling around with his hair.

Reaching up, she used both hands to comb it back from his temples. "Like this?"

He closed his eyes and sighed. "Like that."

"You have wonderful hair." She let the silky strands slip through her fingers. "You should take off your hat when you play guitar."

He kept his eyes closed, as if soaking up her touch. "I like wearing the hat when I play."

"Why?" Moving her hands to his forehead, she traced the path of each eyebrow. His brows were thick, too, and he had long eyelashes. She hadn't noticed that detail until now.

"Protection, I guess."

She didn't have to ask what he meant. Even though she'd never performed for anyone, other than in school plays when she was a little kid, she understood that it had to be somewhat scary unless you were an exhibitionist. Trey wasn't an exhibitionist, which made him vulnerable up there in front of an audience.

Yet he continued to write songs and play them for others. Something in him demanded expression, so he bowed to that demand but kept his hat on. His reason for doing that tugged at her heart.

Leaning forward, she placed a soft kiss on his lips. When she started to pull away, he captured her head in both hands and brought her mouth back to his. "More," he whispered.

She settled into the kiss, stroking his tongue with hers, shifting her angle, finding a better fit, melding her mouth with his, surrendering to the tactile joy of his supple lips. He groaned and thrust his tongue deep.

Without warning her core contracted. She pulled back, gasping. "Stop for a minute."

His dark eyes blazed with fire. "But I like kissing you."

"And I like kissing you, too. A little too much." She took a shaky breath. "I almost came just now."

The heat in his gaze intensified. "Good to know."

"It seems I'm not very talented at this game."

His eyes glittered. "Maybe we should change the rules and see how often I can make you come."

"That's no challenge." Her breathing slowed. "I think I understand the problem. I'm conditioned to come when you and I are naked together."

"Then I should be conditioned that way, too."

"No, because you're a guy. You're conditioned to have an erection whenever we're naked together." She gestured toward his cock. "Exhibit A."

"Can't argue that conclusion."

"But guys, at least the considerate ones, start training themselves to hold off their climaxes, because women tend to take longer. Am I right?"

"Right, except in your case, that's not true. You're a powder keg from the get-go."

"Well, yes and no. I used to take longer. Something about you really flips my switch."

He looked pleased with that information. "So you're saying that with another guy…"

"I would be awesome at this game. But now that you've set up this challenge, I'm determined to meet it."

He frowned. "I'm not sure this is such a good idea, after all. I didn't have the whole picture before, and I like having you conditioned to come whenever you're naked with me."

"But you said my orgasm would be more powerful if I can hold off."

"The *book* said that. But if you're happy with your orgasms as they are, then let's forget this program. The book could be wrong, you know."

He was adorable, and she couldn't remember ever joking around with a man in bed this way. "I *am* happy with my orgasms, but maybe I could be even happier. Come on, Trey. You set up some expectations. No fair abandoning the idea. It might work if I can resist your sexual magnetism."

He laughed. "You are sure good for my ego. I suppose we can have fun trying. So we're back to the original plan?"

"However you wanted to work it is fine with me."

"Then I can kiss you?"

"Sure. I'm ready now." She paused. "What happens after the kissing, so I'm mentally prepared?"

"Caressing above the waist."

"Okay." Her breasts tingled just thinking about that.

"Then caressing below the waist." His tone was casual, but his expression grew more intense.

"I have the advantage there." Moisture gathered between her thighs. "You're more accessible than I am."

"That's a matter of opinion." He surveyed her spread thighs. "You look damned accessible to me."

"No peeking allowed. I'm susceptible to those hot glances."

"Don't think it's only you with an issue. I just found out you're already wet down there. Now I'm harder than ever."

Her breath caught. She was ready to tackle him and forget this nonsense, but he'd aroused her competitive instinct as well as her sexual urges. "That's fair. Ready to start?"

"Oh, yeah."

"On three. One, two, three, *kiss*."

He swooped in. She should have known he'd play dirty. His tongue blatantly mimicked the act they were temporarily avoiding. She gave it right back to him, sucking on his probing tongue and moaning suggestively.

Her reward was listening to his increasingly labored breathing. Or was that her breathing? After a while she couldn't decide who was gasping louder.

She responded to that kiss as usual, which meant she felt the urge to surrender to that great feeling hovering within reach. She fought that urge, which was extremely unfamiliar, but interesting.

He was the one who broke off their kiss, which she scored as a point for her side. When she looked into his heavy-lidded eyes, she could see a battle going on. Chest heaving, he ran his hands over her shoulders in a light massage.

Poor baby. He seemed to be having trouble getting enough air in his lungs. She stroked his shoulders in return, but she used a firm touch. He had muscles that begged for a girl to dig in and appreciate all that manliness.

In spite of having to control her response to him, she liked this routine. She hadn't spent enough time running her hands over his sculpted body, and she was making up for it now. He quivered under her touch.

She glanced into his eyes and saw molten need there. "How're you doing, cowboy?"

A muscle twitched in his jaw. "Just fine. How 'bout you?"

"Fine, just…" Or not. He'd begun to fondle her breasts, and that…that could be trouble. His touch was all the more erotic because of the small calluses on the tips of his fingers. This man could also make a guitar sing with his talented caress, and knowing that excited her even more.

He watched her as he rolled her nipples between his thumb and forefinger. "Your eyes are getting dark."

She didn't doubt it. Her nipples seemed connected to her womb with a taut string, and when he squeezed them gently, it was as if he plucked that string. She began to vibrate.

He had the upper hand now. She would go down in flames unless—unless he was sensitive there, too. Placing both hands over his pecs, she began a slow massage. His heartbeat thudded against her right palm, and when she squeezed his nipples as he'd squeezed hers, the rhythm of his heart picked up.

His hands stilled and his jaw tightened. He closed his eyes and blew out a breath. "That's…good."

"Glad you like it." She continued to stroke his chest and play with his nipples. "You have an incredible body. I love doing this."

He remained motionless, as if she'd mesmerized him with her touch, and perhaps with her voice, too. The idea fascinated her, so she kept talking. "Your skin is like velvet under my fingers, like warm velvet that's been lying in the sun."

His breathing became uneven.

"I'd love to lie naked with you in a sunny meadow and see your skin gleaming in the light, your muscles rippling as you slide into me, your—"

"I want you." His hoarse voice betrayed how much. Tension radiated from him and his whole body trembled with the force of it. "I can't take this. I thought I could, but your voice…" He opened his eyes.

She gasped at the primitive fire in those dark depths. The need reflected there made her shake, too.

He swallowed. "There's a condom on the nightstand."

She'd won. And she'd done it by *talking* to him. Scooting back, she reached for the packet on the nightstand and ripped it open.

"Hurry."

"Yes." She glanced at his cock, where a bead of moisture gathered at the tip. Lowering her head, she licked it off.

"Elle." He grasped her head in both hands, pressing his fingertips into her scalp.

She didn't know if he'd meant to lift her away or urge her down, but in that split second she made her decision. She took him into her mouth and sucked hard.

With a tortured groan, he came, and she took all he gave her. When at last his shudders ceased, she released him, giving him one last intimate kiss.

"Oh, Elle." He lifted her up and pulled her into his lap. "Elle." His mouth found hers.

She wrapped her arms around his neck, and when he urged her thighs apart, she welcomed the firm thrust of his fingers. He caressed her with sure strokes, and the climax she'd resisted so fiercely surged forward with blinding speed. Her hips bucked, and she wrenched her mouth free as the impact of her orgasm left her gasping for air.

He stayed with her, pumping his fingers in and out as she moaned and shook in his arms. She didn't know if it was the best climax ever, but it was pretty damned wonderful. This delayed gratification might be worth exploring some more.

At last she lay still. Slowly she opened her eyes to find him gazing down at her with raw emotion. The intensity of it should probably worry her. But she felt so good, so completely and utterly satisfied, that she couldn't bring herself to be worried about anything.

She gave him a lazy smile. "I win."

9

ELLE HAD WON, all right. Trey knew exactly what she'd won, too—his heart. She'd unknowingly wooed him with her most powerful weapon. Her voice had stayed with him for months, and now he'd never forget it.

Earlier tonight he'd been treated to her honeyed voice speaking in very explicit language that had driven him wild. But that had been child's play compared to what she'd accomplished this time. Her sensual touch and seductive murmurs had woven a spell that had brought him to a fever pitch.

He hadn't merely wanted to have her. He'd wanted to ravage her. Holding himself in check had taken all his strength, and when she'd used her tongue to tease him, his control had snapped. He wasn't sure if she'd meant to finish what she'd started, but he would have given her no choice.

Whether she knew it or not, this level of intimacy had brought them to the soul-baring stage. But he didn't dare tell her that. She seemed to think she was less inhibited with him because they knew so little about each other. Maybe she'd convinced herself that they were having stranger-sex, where the participants were largely anonymous. She couldn't be more wrong.

Without realizing it, she'd already revealed so much. He knew she was both competitive and generous. She was more passionate than any woman he'd had sex with. She didn't back down from a challenge and she used her sense of humor to stay balanced. On top of that, she was honest, at least with him. Maybe not so much with herself.

He'd learned all that from making love to her. Although he didn't know everything about her, he knew enough to recognize someone with the potential to be a lifelong… He hesitated to admit how far his thoughts had taken him. Too far, probably, because she'd given every indication that she wasn't looking for anyone permanent in her life.

He fervently hoped she'd change her mind about that. His strategy would be to love the dickens out of her until she got used to having him around. That would include some old-fashioned wooing, because great as the sex was, they couldn't do it *all* the time.

Consequently, he'd come back to the room tonight prepared with a bottle of wine he'd bought at the bar and the leftover party munchies he'd asked the bartender to package up for him. He gazed into her flushed face. She did look happy. So far, so good. "What do you say to a picnic?"

She laughed and sat up. "I hope you're not suggesting we haul a blanket out into the snow."

"Nope." He thought about the picture she'd painted of lying naked in a meadow. Wrong time of year for that, but he'd remind her of the concept sometime soon. To make that fantasy come true, she'd have to stick around, though. He wasn't sure how well she'd respond to that idea.

"So where will we picnic?"

"Right here. In bed."

"I think we just did that."

"I mean with food and drink."

"Are you going to smear me with cream cheese?"

His cock, which logically should stay at rest for a while, twitched with obvious interest. "Great idea, but I didn't steal any cream cheese from the party. Hold that thought for next time."

"So you're suggesting an actual picnic."

"I am. Are you hungry?"

She tilted her head as if to consider that. "Yes, I am! Must be all the great sex. Whatcha got?"

He climbed out of bed and unearthed his stash, which Fred had packed into a paper bag. Thank God screw-top wine wasn't considered tacky anymore, because he had a bottle of red that wouldn't require a corkscrew. He pulled it out. "You up for this?"

"You bet. I love me a good malbec. But I thought cowboys liked beer."

"I happen to like both, but wine seemed to fit the occasion."

"What occasion?"

Finding you. "Having a chance to be alone and naked together."

"I guess that deserves a toast, now that you mention it. Want me to get us water glasses from the bathroom?"

"I stole glasses, too." He took two stemmed goblets from the bag. "Actually, that's not true. Fred thought I needed them."

"Did Fred know *why* you needed them?"

"Probably." He couldn't see any point in trying to disguise the fact that nearly everyone at the resort assumed he and Elle were getting it on tonight. "Do you care?"

"I'd better not care. The reason I was late involved meeting the Chance brothers and Emmett Sterling in the hallway. I think Jack knew exactly where I was going. Nothing much gets by him."

"That's a fact." Trey took out assorted crackers, pretzels and some chunks of cheese. "Were they all leaving the bachelor party? Is that why you ran into them?"

"They were talking Emmett out of spending the night with his fiancée after she specifically requested that he not do so."

Trey could picture that. He grinned. "Did they succeed?"

"I think so. They were headed up to Emmett's bachelor quarters when I left them. Oh, and Emmett invited me to the wedding and reception."

"He did? Excellent! I was afraid I wouldn't get to see much of you tomorrow. Will you dance with me?" This weekend was improving minute by minute.

"Won't you be playing the music?"

"Not constantly. Watkins and I can trade off, and we'll use some recorded music so we can have a break. We can definitely dance." And he could hardly wait to hold her in his arms on the dance floor. He had a feeling they'd be awesome together there, too.

"That would be fun. Gabe said it will be the wedding of the century."

"A wedding that almost didn't happen. Emmett

wanted to fly to Vegas this afternoon and sabotage the entire effort." Trey spread out napkins on the bed and dumped some of the goodies on them.

"You're kidding!"

"Nope." He accepted the glass of wine she gave him and leaned toward her. "Here's to you, me and a king-size bed."

"I'll drink to that." She touched her goblet to his. "But now tell me more about this Vegas thing. I can't believe it."

Trey carefully positioned himself on the bed so the picnic wouldn't be disturbed. "He's reconsidered that notion."

"Well, I should hope so! Talk about crazy. How could he think of doing such a thing after the preparation and expense?"

"He's not into all that. And Pam's money is paying for it."

"Oh." She nibbled on some cheese. "I did wonder where the money was coming from. I thought maybe the Chance family was footing the bill."

"No. If they were organizing things, they'd probably have suggested having it at the ranch instead. Pam was the one behind coming to the resort. She wanted everyone to get away from their place of work so they'd feel free to party."

"Makes sense." She picked up a cracker. "Great eats, Trey. Thanks."

"You're welcome." He added a sense of gratitude to her list of good qualities.

"I looked up the Last Chance on the internet tonight."

"You did?" He found that very encouraging. "What did you think?"

"It's gorgeous."

"The place is even prettier than it looks online. Dominique took some awesome pictures for the website, but nothing beats actually being there, working in that historic barn, training the registered paints they breed. I was really happy to get the job." He drank some wine while he thought about whether he should say what was on his mind. Aw, hell, why not? "You should come out and see it for yourself."

She studied him over the rim of her glass. "Why?"

Because I want you to fall in love with my world, and with me, that's why. He couldn't say that, either. He was censoring himself a lot, and he wondered how long his tolerance for that would hold out. "It's a landmark in Jackson Hole. Now that you've met the owners, you might as well take a look at the place, just to say you've been there."

"I'll keep that in mind." She picked up a cracker, put some cheese on it and popped it in her mouth.

He had trouble not focusing all his attention on her, which she wouldn't appreciate. But she looked so cute sitting on the bed with no clothes on, sipping her wine and eating her snack. He stored the image away. There was a chance this was all he'd ever have, and he needed to be realistic about that.

She finished her cracker and cheese. "Do you ever play guitar at the Spirits and Spurs?"

"I have, a time or two. Where did you hear about that place?"

"Jared mentioned it. He spends the summers here in Jackson Hole. God knows what he does to keep himself occupied and solvent all summer. He must pick up odd jobs. But apparently sometimes he drops in at the Spirits and Spurs in Shoshone." She drank more wine. "Do you think it's really haunted?"

He realized that she was intrigued by the ranch and the nearby town, but he didn't want to overplay his hand. She'd been motivated to check out the area on-line, but that could have been idle curiosity. It didn't mean she was ready to give up her summers in Argentina to be here. Or to be with him.

"I've never seen a ghost," he said. "I've never even sensed a ghostly presence. But I know those who have. Some think that Archie Chance, the Chance brothers' grandfather, shows up at the Spirits and Spurs from time to time. They say he used to hang out at the bar whenever his wife, Nelsie, went shopping in town."

"Probably no ghosts make an appearance in winter, though."

"Sure they do. Remember the story of Scrooge?"

"Oh, yeah." She looked thoughtful. "I admit to being fascinated by the idea of ghosts. I don't really believe in them, but still…"

He set his wineglass on the nightstand. "Elle, if you have the slightest interest in going to the Spirits and Spurs, I'll take you. I can't promise ghosts, but Josie decorates it real nice for the holidays. Not like Serenity, of course. But nice."

"Serenity's a little over the top, but I like it."

"Spirits and Spurs decorations are a lot simpler. There's a tree, and pine boughs and twinkling lights. Well, and Josie always hangs up mistletoe. She claims the customers expect it, but I think she's the one who likes it, personally."

"Maybe the mistletoe attracts ghosts."

"Maybe."

Elle looked eager for a moment, as if she might be considering his invitation. But then her expression changed and she shrugged. "I usually stick around here during the holidays so Jared and Annalise can have time off. I'll need to work."

"Even at night? Every night?"

"We have night skiing for the more experienced guests. Don't worry about it. Christmas is no big deal for me, really."

"You're not into Christmas?"

"There's not much point, in my case. I buy gifts for my parents and send them to wherever they're currently stationed, and a cousin and I exchange presents every year, but that's the extent of my involvement."

He didn't know what to say to that without prying into her personal business. Obviously seeing her folks during the holidays wasn't important to her. Mentioning that his folks weren't alive anymore so he had nowhere special to go during the holidays would be an unnecessary downer.

His special place was quickly becoming the Last Chance. He'd heard from Watkins all about how the family celebrated. Watkins loved holidays at the ranch. Consequently, Trey was really looking forward to Christmas Eve, when the Chances invited all the hands to the house for a big party. Christmas Day was nice, too, according to Watkins, because anyone was welcome to drop in from noon on, after the family members had opened presents and finished their Christmas breakfast.

Elle drained her glass. "More wine?"

"Sure, why not?" He finished his wine and held out his glass.

"It's good stuff."

"Not bad." He took a long swallow. "You know what? We should toast Emmett and Pam. Without them, we wouldn't be here."

"Good point. And I'm even going to the wedding tomorrow." She leaned over and clicked the rim of her glass against his. "To Emmett and Pam." She glanced at his arm as he raised his glass to his lips. "Trey, I promised myself I wouldn't ask you about your tattoo, but it's late, and we've had sex and wine, and I keep staring at it whenever you flex your arm."

He tried to ignore the sense of foreboding. Things were going so well, but this wasn't a topic he wanted to discuss yet. "Why do you suppose I have a tattoo? It's so ladies will fixate on my manly muscles."

"I've heard that's why guys get tattoos there."

"You've heard right."

"But why an angel wing?"

His pulse rate spiked. How to answer? "I needed a tattoo and I liked it better than the hula girl."

"I don't believe that's the reason. You're not the type to pick some random thing and have it inked on your body, not even to get women."

"How do you know I'm not?"

"Because… Well, I just know, that's all."

So she wasn't going to admit that she'd learned important things about him, too. Of course she had. They couldn't have been so intimate without her picking up on facets of his personality.

He thought about lying and saying that it was a generic symbol of his guardian angel. He wasn't in the habit of lying, but he didn't think she'd like hearing the truth. They had a fragile understanding, one that could be easily shattered.

But he had hopes for this relationship, fragile though it might be. Lying about his tattoo would be something he couldn't fix if they ended up together. Eventually he'd have to tell her why he had it, and then he'd be exposed as a liar.

So he chose to tell her the truth and accept the consequences. "As I mentioned before, I tried to find you after you saved me last spring."

Her expression turned wary. "Right."

"When I couldn't find you, I needed...*wanted*...to commemorate that lifesaving moment. I thought of you as my angel. Well, *an* angel, not necessarily *my* angel. So I got the tattoo."

Wariness had turned to shock. "So the tattoo is for *me?*"

"I needed something, Elle, something to express my gratitude for being alive, and your part in it. I chose this. It represents a twist of fate as much as anything."

She didn't seem to be buying that. "I'm not an angel, Trey. I'm so far from being an angel it's hysterically funny. I spew four-letter words when I have sex with you!"

"That's not the point." He reached for her, but she leaped off the bed.

"I think it's exactly the point. You've created some idealized image of the person who rescued you. She's an effing *angel*. Her wing is now a permanent part of your body!"

"I did that before I knew you." He left the bed, desperate for her to understand. "I wasn't even sure you were real! For all I knew, you were some heavenly being who'd swooped down to make sure I didn't die!"

"I am real, Trey." She picked up her yoga pants. "And human and fallible. I make mistakes all the time. One of them might be getting involved with you."

"Don't say that."

"I said *might*." She pulled on her pants. "The jury's still out on the question. But my initial impression, when I heard you calling out for your girlfriend, Cassie, was that you were a romantic soul who needed to find an equally romantic soul." She located her jacket on the floor.

He wanted to argue with her about being a romantic, but he thought she could be right. Who else but a romantic would have an angel wing tattooed on his arm? Who else would write a song about the angel who had saved him, and then actually perform it for other folks?

So, if they were ever going to have a future, which seemed less likely now than it had five minutes ago, she'd have to accept that about him. "Maybe I *am* a romantic guy," he said. "If I have that tendency, I've tried to downplay it because I sensed that wouldn't impress you."

"You've got that right." She zipped her jacket. "Sappy sentimentality doesn't work for me."

"Ouch."

"Sorry." She scanned the floor looking for her shoes. "That was a little harsh."

"It was a lot harsh. Is that how you see me? A sentimental sap?"

"No. At least not mostly." She found the shoes. "We've had some good, honest sex that wasn't sentimental at all. I'm on board with that. But when I discover that the angel's wing on your arm represents me, I get worried. You're expecting something from me that I'm not prepared to give." She shoved her feet into the shoes.

"Yet."

She whirled to face him. "What the hell does that mean?"

"Don't forget that I've made love to you, Elle. I've known you in a way that you may not even admit to yourself. There's a depth of feeling you may not acknowledge, but I feel it. Damn it, I was there, holding you, and I felt it!"

She gazed at him. "You're delusional." Then she turned and walked out of his room, closing the door quietly behind her.

He wished she'd slammed it. That, at least, would have shown some fiery emotion. He knew she had it in her. He'd experienced it firsthand.

But she was willing to pretend that her ordered life had no room for that kind of passion. He scared her because he threatened to upset the careful image she'd created of how things should be.

He didn't blame her for being confused. Although he had to read between the lines, he could guess that she'd been taught not to get attached to people or places. That might have been a by-product of being a kid with parents in the military, but he'd known others with that background and they weren't so fiercely independent.

The clue might be her lack of interest in seeing her parents for Christmas. Hell, if he still had parents, he'd make damn sure he traveled to wherever they were.

But she might have been taught through example to minimize the importance of family celebrations.

She'd told him that his emotional response to losing Cassie had kept her from maintaining contact. But although she tried to present herself as a person who didn't need those messy emotions, her joyful response to having sex with him said otherwise. He suspected she was hungry for a deep personal connection.

Maybe she'd sensed that she was making one with him and had panicked. He could go after her, calm her down. Instead, he decided to sit tight and see if she could stay away. He was hoping that she couldn't.

10

ELLE HAD A bad feeling she'd overreacted. But she needed time to think, and she couldn't think very well when in the presence of Trey's magnificently naked body, especially decorated with that exceedingly sentimental tattoo. Thankfully no one was in the halls as she hurried back to her room.

Once there, she went to switch on her bedside lamp and changed her mind. Instead, she turned on her Christmas tree lights. Then she flopped down on her bed and lay there surrounded by the soft, multicolored glow.

It reminded her of a Christmas many years ago, one she'd spent with her parents in Germany. She'd been in third grade, so she would have been eight. She'd begged for a tree that year, as she had every year.

They'd never had one, or even much in the way of decorations. Her mother had insisted that hauling ornaments around from place to place was ridiculous. Neither was she willing to buy new ones each time and discard them when they moved, because that would be wasteful.

When her mom hadn't budged that year, either, Elle had used money she'd been saving for a bike and bought a tree, a stand and ornaments. It hadn't been a very big tree, but she'd put it up in a fit of rebellion, determined that she'd enjoy the heck out of it.

That hadn't been easy when her parents had both made her feel silly for doing such a thing. They'd acted as if the tree was a nuisance, and she'd been told to take it down the day after Christmas. Putting it up and taking it down by herself had been a lot of work, and when they'd moved, her parents hadn't wanted to take the ornaments. In the end, she'd given them to a friend at school.

She'd always assumed her parents, especially her mother, were simply being practical. Now she wondered if that was the whole story. Neither of them made a big deal out of anything tradition-oriented, come to think of it. Not birthdays or anniversaries, either.

Elle had accepted their lack of interest in celebrating, along with the idea that wasting time and money on such things made no sense. They would laugh if they knew Pam Mulholland had rented out an entire ski resort for her wedding to Emmett Sterling. Elle saw something of her parents' attitude in Emmett.

What a shame it would have been if he'd succeeded in ruining this for his fiancée. Elle had always identified with the Emmett Sterlings of the world, but tonight, to her surprise, she found herself siding with Pam. If a sixty-something woman wanted to use her money to celebrate marrying the man she loved, why not?

How all that tied in with Trey was unclear right

now, but Elle would go to the wedding. She was very interested in seeing how Emmett adjusted to his bride's need to mark the occasion with public joy and extravagance. And Elle would dance with Trey if he still wanted her to. With that thought, she left the Christmas lights on, which was completely impractical and wasteful, and drifted off to sleep.

THE NEXT DAY she estimated that she'd probably spent more time dressing for the wedding than the bride herself. Because she traveled between Jackson Hole and Argentina every year, she kept her wardrobe simple. Yet she wanted to look good. No, not just *good*. She wanted to look amazing.

That left her with one choice—a cobalt-blue, knee-length jersey dress that could be dressed up or down. Today's event called for dressing it up, so she added a hammered silver necklace with large, irregularly shaped links, and earrings with the same type of asymmetrical loops. Her open-toed silver stilettos hardly ever came out of the closet, but now was the time.

She'd spent a good twenty minutes on her makeup, and she'd piled her hair on top of her head and secured it with several rhinestone hairpins. The glitter might be a bit much for an afternoon wedding, but she expected the reception to last into the night. She rummaged through her drawers and found the silver clutch she'd bought to match the stilettos.

Her small, utilitarian room didn't have a full-length mirror, so she could only see herself from her hips up. That much looked okay, so she'd assume the rest passed muster, too. As she walked down the stairs and into the guest area of the resort, she realized the dress code for a ranch foreman's wedding might be Western formal. Oh, well. She didn't own anything that fit that description.

The mellow sound of guitar music beckoned her to the room where the wedding was being held. Her stomach churned at the thought of seeing Trey again. Their night together hadn't ended well, mostly because of her.

He hadn't tried to contact her since then, even though they had each other's cell numbers. She'd reminded herself that he was no doubt busy with wedding activities, but that argument didn't wash. He was the guitarist for the ceremony and the reception, not a member of the wedding party.

That meant he could have texted or called this morning. He hadn't, but then she hadn't contacted him, either. Frankly, she didn't know what to say. She still worried that he'd created a fantasy that she could never live up to.

When she thought of him having his arm tattooed to commemorate her rescuing him, she shivered. Getting tattooed hurt, or so she'd been told. Maybe he'd done it after several shots of hard liquor, but still. He'd subjected himself to the process in her honor.

She didn't know what to do with that information. Her parents, the people who'd given her life, hadn't done much of anything for her major life events. Graduations were taken in stride, and when she'd won skiing competitions, they'd phoned to say it was nice. No flowers, no card.

Trey had allowed someone to stick needles under his skin and permanently alter his appearance because he believed she deserved to be honored. Not *her,* exactly, but the idea of her, the angelic vision he carried of that rescue. The guy was adorable, and wow, could he do the horizontal mambo, but the tattoo thing was intense.

She wasn't quite sure what to make of it. Even so, she yearned to see him, to be with him, to hold him close. He was Trey, the sexy guy who'd given her orgasms she wasn't likely to forget anytime soon. He was also fun, and caring and honest.... He could have lied to her about the tattoo. She gave him props for not doing that.

A sweet-looking redhead who couldn't be more than eighteen sat at a table just inside the door with a guest book in front of her. She looked up when Elle approached. "What a gorgeous dress!"

"Thank you. I'm Elle Masterson. I'm a ski instructor here. I don't know if Emmett had time to mention that he invited me, but I—"

"I know *exactly* who you are, Ms. Masterson." Her blue eyes shone with excitement. "You're the lady who rescued Trey Wheeler." The girl held out her hand. "I'm Cassidy O'Connelli. My sister Morgan is married to Gabe Chance, and my sister Tyler is married to Alex Keller. You gave Alex and Gabe ski lessons yesterday. Everyone had a blast!"

"Good! I didn't see you out there yesterday. Don't you like to ski?"

"I've never tried it, but I might tomorrow. Pam needed me to help her with a few things, and that was fine with me. I love weddings. I'm apprenticing to be the new housekeeper at the Last Chance. You should come and visit."

"Thanks." The blizzard of information from Cassidy combined with soft guitar music left Elle feeling distracted. She did her best to focus on Cassidy when all she really wanted to do was check out Trey's guitar performance. "I appreciate the invitation, and I'll try to make it out there."

"I hope you do. Here comes Jeb. He'll escort you to your seat."

Elle smiled at the freckle-faced cowboy who'd been one of her students the day before. He wore a smart-looking Western coat, a white shirt and a bolo tie. "Hi, Jeb. You're looking good."

Jeb offered his arm. "Pam wanted all of us to be stylin', so she helped pick out our clothes. I get to keep the jacket."

"Bonus."

"I *know*. I've never owned a jacket this nice. You're sitting on the groom's side, right?"

"I guess so. Emmett's the one who invited me."

"Then I'm putting you on the groom's side. Isn't this the fanciest wedding you've ever seen?"

"It's pretty fancy." To please Jeb, she glanced around at the greenery, wine-colored ribbons and white roses. Tiny white lights twinkled everywhere. Wine-colored poinsettias were clustered on tiered stands around the perimeter of the room.

"It's like a fairyland," Jeb said. "Well, here you go. This is your seat." He indicated a spot on the aisle in the fourth row. "You're gonna love this wedding. It'll be awesome. And cute. Little Archie, Jack's son, and Sara Bianca, Gabe's daughter, will be in it. And by the way, you look beautiful."

"What a nice thing to say. Thank you, Jeb."

"It's the truth. Oh, here's your program." He handed her an elegantly printed booklet. "If you'll excuse me, I have more people to escort."

"You go right ahead. I'll be fine." She would be more than fine in this spot. At last she had what she wanted—an excellent view of Trey. He and Watkins sat to the left of a greenery-covered arch that would serve as the focal point for the ceremony. Trey was not wearing his hat.

Watkins wasn't wearing one, either, so Pam might have made a no-hats decision. In any case, Elle loved being able to see Trey's expression as he played a gentle love ballad.

Although neither man was singing, Elle had no trouble filling in the lyrics. She knew the song well. She'd bet Trey did, too, and was repeating them in his head as he played. Watkins might be a better guitarist, especially because he'd had more years of practice, but in Elle's completely biased opinion, Trey put more emotion into the notes.

She'd been an idiot to ever think he could carry on an affair without becoming involved. He was an artist. Artists had to give rein to their emotions, whereas she was a ski instructor, an analytical teacher. She'd been raised by parents who believed in logic and efficiency. She believed in those things, too. Didn't she?

If so, she wasn't doing a very good job of being logical and efficient regarding Trey. Her breath caught as she watched him strum his guitar. Less than twelve hours ago, those strong fingers had been touching her, loving her, making her moan. She squirmed in her seat. She wanted him to make love to her again.

But was that fair to Trey? She'd been right all along.

He needed someone as romantic as he was, someone who would send him sentimental love notes and appreciate his flair for the dramatic. Speaking of that, how would he explain his tattoo to a future lover?

Although it was unworthy of her, she liked the idea that he'd have to. Perhaps he shouldn't have honored her with that angel's wing, but he couldn't do much about it now. Like it or not, he was stuck with this memory of her. That shouldn't make her smile. But it did.

The room gradually filled with happy people. Elle could feel the good cheer in the air, hear it in the muted laughter, see it in the glowing expressions and wide smiles. This was why Pam had insisted on a public celebration. It was a gift to all those who knew her and Emmett, all those who wanted to share in their joy.

But Elle couldn't help wondering how Emmett was holding up. About that time, he entered from a side door, accompanied by Jack, Gabe and Nick. Those brothers made an impressive trio, but Emmett was the guy Elle focused on.

She need not have worried about him. He looked magnificent. Tall and silver-haired, he carried himself with pride and assurance, as if he'd decided that this was, in fact, the most glorious day of his life so far, and he planned to enjoy it to the fullest.

Elle wasn't sure what she'd expected—maybe a hesitant man who had to be bolstered by the three younger cowboys at his side. Instead, he took the leadership role, and they served as his trusty companions.

Elle knew all would be well. Emmett had risen to the occasion and would make his bride proud. She barely knew Emmett and didn't know Pam at all, but her understanding of Emmett's dilemma had given her a stake in the proceedings. Happy anticipation made her glance in Trey's direction.

As if they'd choreographed it, he was looking back. He and Watkins had finished the last of the preceremony numbers, and Trey sat with his guitar in his lap and his gaze trained on her. He wasn't smiling. Her heart stuttered. Did he think their interlude was over?

She wouldn't blame him if he thought that. All things considered, he'd probably be better off without her. Selfish person that she was, she didn't want to let him go. Not yet. But perhaps he'd decided she wasn't worth the trouble.

Watkins leaned over and murmured something to Trey. With one last glance at Elle, he settled his guitar more firmly against his thighs. Together, he and Watkins began to play the "Wedding March."

The guests rose and turned toward the back of the room. So did Elle, which meant she couldn't see Trey anymore. But she was here for a wedding, and Pam deserved to be honored after all she'd gone through to plan this event.

Elle didn't know what to expect. It was doubtful that Pam's father was alive and could walk her down the aisle, and the three Chance brothers were all at the altar with Emmett.

First a little flower girl appeared. Her red hair indicated she was Morgan and Gabe Chance's daughter, Sarah Bianca. Basket of rose petals in hand, she surveyed the admiring crowd like the princess she undoubtedly thought she was in her frothy emerald dress and crown of rosebuds.

And no wonder. She was adorable, and every camera was pointed in her direction. Behind her, though, some fuss was going on.

Standing on tiptoe, Elle could see Josie Chance, elegant in a long blue dress, urging a small blond boy down the aisle behind Sarah Bianca. Elle pegged this tyke as Josie and Jack's son, Archie, the designated ring bearer. He was tricked out in a Western vest, coat, pants and tiny boots, but he seemed totally uninterested in his assignment.

With a martyred sigh, Sarah Bianca turned around and grabbed his hand. Then she proceeded to tow him down the aisle while he kept stopping to gaze in wonder at his surroundings. She wouldn't allow it. Her jaw was set and her attention was fixed on the goal.

Good thing the rings were tied to the pillow, because Archie clutched it to his chest like a favorite teddy bear. Deprived of a free hand to toss rose petals, Sarah Bianca swung the basket vigorously so they'd spill out behind her. She had everything under control.

Chuckles rippled through the gathering, but no one laughed out loud. That impressed Elle. Apparently everyone here recognized that Sarah Bianca was struggling to make things right the best way she knew how. That was worthy of admiration, not ridicule. These were good people.

Josie managed to keep her composure, too, as she followed the pair. Elle could see the combination of laughter and tears swimming in her eyes, but she took a deep breath and kept going.

Morgan Chance appeared next. She obviously was fighting the same battle to keep from both laughing and crying at the antics of her daughter and Josie's son. This, Elle knew, would be a moment talked about for many years.

Elle wondered if Dominique Chance, Nick's wife, would be next down the aisle, but then she noticed a movement at the front of the aisle. There was Dominique crouching down, camera in hand, as little Archie broke away from his cousin and ran to his father.

Jack scooped him up with a grin. It looked as if Jack would hold on to him during the ceremony, which also meant the rings would be available when needed. Dominique captured it all.

Elle could imagine how great those pictures would be, considering Dominique's photography skills. Maybe Dominique would preview them at the reception, or put some up on a website. Elle decided to ask about that later.

When a soft murmur passed through the group, Elle faced the back of the room again. At last, Pam stood in the doorway wearing a stunning burgundy velvet gown. On her left side was a blonde woman whose bone structure hinted that she might be related to Emmett. Elle guessed she might be his daughter. On Pam's other side stood a silver-haired woman with a regal bearing who could only be Sarah Chance, matriarch of the Chance family.

Elle loved it. No man was going to give this woman to her dashing ranch foreman. No, the women of the Last Chance owned this rite of passage. Elle, who was only barely acquainted with them, felt a moment of solidarity as they passed. She resisted the urge to give them a high five.

Once Pam and her companions had gone by, Elle turned to watch the bride approach her broad-shouldered groom. His eyes shone, and she moved toward him with the steady gait of a woman certain of her path. Elle's throat tightened and her eyes grew moist. She couldn't remember the last time she'd cried, but she was crying now.

God, it was beautiful, this joining of two lives, this celebration of all things precious between them. Tears slid down her cheeks. Someday…when she was ready…when she'd tired of the freedom to move unfettered about the world….

But that time had not come, she reminded herself gently. She was viewing an image of what was to be in the future. She shouldn't get too carried away by the emotional ceremony taking place today.

She wouldn't wait until she was in her sixties before she looked for a guy, but she had more to see and do. She'd given herself at least until she was thirty before settling down, which was more than two years away. She didn't want to jump the gun.

That was important to remember whenever she interacted with Trey. Most people had a mental timetable, whether they acknowledged it or not. His wasn't in sync with hers.

But thanks to him, she had begun examining the patterns she'd been taught as a child. Thanks to him, she'd discovered a capacity for pleasure that she'd never dreamed of having. Thanks to him, she was able to be part of a celebration that showed her that sometimes, pulling out all the stops could be wonderful.

The ceremony was classy and relatively short. It included one musical interlude when Tyler Keller sang, accompanied by Watkins and Trey. Emmett and Pam promised to love and cherish each other, and when they kissed, everyone in the room cheered.

Grinning like teenagers, the newly married couple hurried back down the aisle accompanied by lively guitar music. The guests streamed after them, bound for a reception in the ballroom down the hall. Everyone, that was, except Elle and Mary Lou, Watkins's wife.

When Elle noticed that Mary Lou was waiting for Watkins, she decided to take her cue and wait for Trey. No one had to know that she and Trey had exchanged sharp words the last time they'd seen each other.

Mary Lou motioned for Elle to come and stand with her. "Weren't our guys terrific?"

"They were."

"Tyler and Watkins made a recording last year, and Josie sells the CD at the Spirits and Spurs. I think they should make another one, don't you?"

"That's a great idea."

"I'm so glad Emmett invited you. I'm sure Trey was thrilled you could come."

"I hope so." She planned to act as if they had nothing to quarrel about. This wouldn't be the time to talk about the issues, anyway. But she couldn't completely ignore their less-than-happy parting. He was too much of a gentleman to reject her in front of Mary Lou and Watkins, but he might after they reached the reception.

He walked toward her, his guitar case in one hand. "Glad you came." He still wasn't smiling.

"I wouldn't have missed it. You and Watkins were wonderful."

"Thanks. It was fun."

She lowered her voice. "Trey, I'm so sor—"

"Never mind." He hooked his free arm around her waist and drew her in for a quick kiss. "We'll talk later."

"Good." She hoped they'd do a whole lot more than talk.

"You look amazing, Elle."

She sighed. "Thank you." It would be all right. Because he had a big heart, he'd forgiven her for running out on him and saying a few things she wished she could take back. But somehow she had to figure out how to keep from breaking that big heart of his. That would be a challenge.

_11_

WHEN ELLE HAD walked in, Trey had screwed up a chord, but he'd quickly recovered and didn't think anybody but Watkins had noticed. Then she'd actually waited for him to pack up so she could go over to the reception with him. He wasn't sure what it all meant, or what exactly she'd been about to apologize for, but at least she was here.

If she'd planned to tell him she was sorry, but it was over between them, he wasn't about to give her that opportunity. He couldn't let her break up with him before he danced with her. Dancing was bound to help his cause, especially if they moved as well together as he expected they would.

Amy had said Elle was susceptible to his music, so he'd use that during the reception, too. He'd grab every chance to convince her that throwing away something this great was a crime against nature. He'd use sex, too, because she responded well to that.

She'd admitted that she'd never had it this good. He wondered if she'd asked herself why that was. Sure, people talked about having great sex with a virtual stranger, but how often did that happen? In his view, the best sex took place between two people who were right for each other in many ways. Right for each other like Pam and Emmett were, for example.

"How did you like the wedding?" he asked as they walked hand-in-hand, following Watkins and Mary Lou down the hall to the reception.

"Loved it."

"Me, too. Everything went off like clockwork. I was worried that Emmett wouldn't throw himself into the occasion, but he was a stand-up guy in the end. He came through with flying colors."

"He did! He looked so proud and handsome at the altar. Maybe he finally realized how special the moment was, and how important it was to experience that moment with family and friends. Vegas would have been so…impersonal."

"Vegas would have been a disaster. Besides, Watkins said Pam would never have agreed to Vegas. He thinks she would have called off the wedding before she'd have agreed to get married there."

Watkins glanced over his shoulder. "Did I hear my name mentioned?"

"I was just telling Elle your opinion about how Pam would have reacted if Emmett had insisted on Vegas."

"Oh, he's right." Mary Lou paused and glanced back at them. "I talked to Sarah, who said that Pam was breathing fire over that suggestion. Good thing Trey changed Emmett's mind."

"Trey?" Elle glanced at him. "I didn't realize you were the magician who made this come out okay."

"It wasn't just me. Watkins said some good things, too."

"No, it was you." Watkins and Mary Lou turned around, and Watkins lowered his voice. "You helped Emmett understand why Mary Lou wasn't backing him up on the Vegas idea. That was the key."

Mary Lou directed her comments to Elle. "Emmett expected my support because Watkins and I got married on a cruise instead of at the ranch."

"Oh." After seeing how much everyone enjoyed this wedding, Elle was surprised.

"Which was fine." Watkins obviously wanted to demonstrate his loyalty to Mary Lou.

"It was fine," she said. "I didn't want a fuss, and it wasn't like we were young folks, like you two, for example."

Elle flinched. She hoped Mary Lou wasn't making assumptions.

"However…" Mary Lou exchanged a meaningful glance with her husband. "We probably should have gotten married at the ranch, shared the occasion with everyone and then gone on the cruise."

"Probably," Watkins said.

"It doesn't matter how old you are." Mary Lou sighed. "People want to be there, and now I understand why. I would have been devastated if Pam and Emmett had run off somewhere to get married."

"We could renew our vows," Watkins said.

"Excellent idea," Trey said. "I volunteer to play for it."

Mary Lou brightened. "That does sound like fun. Except aren't you supposed to do that for a significant anniversary? We haven't been married that long."

"Lou-Lou, every anniversary with you is significant."

"Aw. You are so full of it." But Mary Lou smiled and kissed him on the cheek. "We'll do it next summer, then." She turned to Elle. "And you should come."

"I'd love to, but I'll be in Argentina all summer."

"Really? All summer?" Mary Lou looked over at Trey. "That's a long way from Jackson Hole."

"Yep." Trey didn't need anyone to tell him that. He wasn't ready to accept the idea that Elle would go to Argentina in April. He wasn't planning to accept it until he had no choice. "Hey, we'd better get in there and start playing before the natives get restless."

Watkins nodded. "Right. We can plan our summer party later. Pam's expecting music at this shindig, and we're all she's got, poor lady."

"She's got the best," Mary Lou said. "Isn't that so, Elle?"

"It certainly is." Elle gave Trey a big smile. "Go on in there and do your stuff, cowboy. We'll both be watching."

He liked that big ol' smile of hers. He just wished she hadn't also reminded him that she intended to leave for Argentina as planned. He'd heard of relationships working out when the two people were separated for months at a time, but he'd never been a fan of the concept.

Once they entered the reception, Trey had to focus the bulk of his attention on entertaining the wedding guests. Dancing was a big deal at the Last Chance, and most everyone wanted danceable tunes. Trey and Watkins played and sang, joined every so often by Tyler.

While he was stuck on the makeshift bandstand, Trey had to put up with watching Elle dance with other guys. But he couldn't expect her to sit on the sidelines and wait for him to take a break. She looked good out there, but he reacted to having anyone holding her besides him.

Then someone asked him to play the song he'd written for Elle. "I'll have to ask the lady if it's okay," he said. "Don't want to embarrass her."

"Too late!" Elle called out.

That got a laugh, but he didn't consider her comment to be permission. Looking at her, he held out his fist, thumb pointed sideways. He hoped she understood what he was asking.

She must have, because she mimicked his gesture and turned her thumb up. He was more pleased than she could imagine. Although he'd love to serenade her with this song, he wouldn't have done it if she'd said no.

Settling down on the stool next to the microphone, he began strumming his guitar. The words had come to him so quickly the night he'd written them. No song had been this easy to write.

Holding her gaze, he sang to her about being lost and without hope. Then she'd come out of the darkness, his angel. He had to agree with her that the lyrics were sappy, but that was why he loved them. She'd saved his life, and if a guy couldn't get sentimental because a beautiful woman had come to his rescue, then why write songs at all?

Even from this distance he could see her cheeks turn pink. She was embarrassed, but she hadn't looked away. Not once. Instead, her attention had locked onto him as if they were connected by an invisible cord.

He milked the moment for all it was worth. If Amy was right, and Elle had a soft spot for country singers, then he'd work it. Her love of country music was another dead giveaway that she wasn't the hard-boiled realist she pretended to be. Country music was full of schmaltz.

At the end of the song, the crowd seemed to be holding its breath, as if everyone needed a second or two to absorb the last notes. He liked that. It was the sign of a good tune. Standing, he gazed at Elle, who continued to stand as motionless as a carved statue.

He blew her a kiss, and the room erupted in applause, whistles and stomping feet. Finally, in the midst of the commotion, she broke eye contact with him and ducked her head. But not before he saw her smile.

He propped his guitar in its stand and glanced at Watkins. "Can you take it for the next number? And make it a waltz?"

Watkins winked at him and covered his mike. "You got it, Romeo." Then he uncovered his mike again. "Tyler Keller, would you come on up and sing for us? At the request of my partner, I'm gonna treat you folks to a waltz, and Tyler sings a mighty pretty version of 'If I Didn't Have You in My World.'"

Perfect song, Trey thought as he climbed down from the temporary stage and moved through the crowd in search of Elle. Along the way people shook his hand and slapped him on the back. No doubt they thought he'd made a conquest by performing that tune of his, but he wasn't taking any bets on that. Elle was a tough nut to crack.

He didn't have to go far to find her. She was standing at the edge of the dance floor waiting for him. Her blue eyes sparkled as she stepped toward him. "I assume this is our dance?"

"If you'll do me the honor."

"I've been looking forward to it."

"Me, too." He drew her into his arms as Tyler began to sing. And the world slipped away. There was only Elle, moving with him as he'd known she would.

He breathed in her scent, a subtle flowery one that he didn't recognize. Maybe it was something she put on her hair when she fixed it this way. He leaned down and brushed his lips over her exposed neck.

"You'd better be careful," she murmured. "I'm a ticking time bomb."

"Oh?" He nuzzled her again. He didn't mind making her crazy. That seemed only fair, because holding her this close was making him crazy, too.

"I mean it, Trey. You are one sexy dude up on that stage. I keep watching you fingering your guitar strings. It gets me hot."

He whirled her around, and she followed him perfectly. "You like the way I finger my strings?"

She gazed up at him. "You know I do."

"Nice to hear. Do you have plans after this shindig is over?"

"I hope so. Do you?"

"I hope so." He looked into her eyes and wondered if she was listening to the lyrics of "If I Didn't Have You in My World." "Nice tune."

"Did you request it?"

"No."

"I wouldn't put it past you."

"I didn't think that far ahead. I just asked for a

waltz. Watkins decided on that one, but I agree with
his choice. It fits."

"Tyler sings it well."

"Mmm." He spun her around again. "Argentina,
huh?"

"That's the plan."

He didn't comment on that, but he nuzzled her neck
again, just because he could. Her small whimper made
him smile. She might think she was going to Argentina, but that was because he hadn't pulled out all the
stops yet.

ELLE COULDN'T DENY that Trey was one virile cowboy.
And she hadn't even seen him on a horse yet. After
their dance, which had added another sexy arrow to
the guy's quiver, he'd returned to the bandstand.

She'd spent more time than she'd like to admit sur-
reptitiously observing his long fingers moving up and
down the slender neck of his guitar. There was no better word for it—he fondled that instrument, using both
quick and slow movements that brought back vivid
memories of how he'd touched her.

The wedding guests enthusiastically applauded the
guitarists. They loved the added dimension of Tyler's
vocals. They wanted more.

A buffet was laid out and the liquor flowed. Elle
didn't begrudge anyone this celebration, especially
Pam and Emmett, who seemed to be having more fun
than anyone. But she wanted to be alone with Trey.

He and Watkins finished a rousing tune that had
everyone line dancing, and then Watkins spoke into
his mike. "Folks, we're going to take a break and get
something to eat. Our former professional DJ, Alex

Keller, has agreed to keep you company while we do that, and he's taking requests. We'll be back shortly."

As Elle wondered what constituted "shortly," Trey appeared by her side.

"Fill us a couple of plates while I get us something to drink. I'll meet you out in the hall in five minutes."

She didn't have to be asked twice. Looping the short strap of her clutch purse over her wrist, she crossed to the buffet table. Finger food seemed like the best choice, so she went with that—chilled shrimp, tiny quiches and elaborate petits fours.

Once she had two plates piled high, she made her way through the crowd and used her hip to open one of the double doors. Trey was already there, leaning against the wall looking gorgeous as he held two flutes of champagne.

"I hope you like the bubbly stuff. It was the quickest to grab."

"I like bubbly stuff. It fits the mood. Did you want to sit on the floor?"

"Hell, no. We're going to my room. We can make it there in a couple of minutes if we move fast."

"Okay, but I'm not sure that's a good idea." She fell into step beside him and walked as quickly as her stilettos would allow.

"Why not?"

"I'm liable to jump your bones."

"God, I hope so."

That made her laugh, which wasn't the best way to get two loaded plates of food transported quickly down the hallway and through the lobby. Her little purse swung wildly from her wrist, and a couple of cherry tomatoes bounced onto the carpet. "I'm dropping food."

"Ask me if I care."

"You don't want this food?"

"I'll cram a little of it down my throat after I've done what I've wanted to do for hours."

Her pulse hammered. "Lie down?"

"I don't care. We can lie, or sit or stand up, just so my cock is securely inside you."

She glanced around, but no one was in the hallway, thank goodness. "You might want to keep it down."

"I've been trying to keep it down for quite some time, and the damned thing keeps rising up on me whenever I look at you in that dress."

"This dress? There's nothing particularly suggestive about it!"

"That's what you think. There's just enough cleavage to remind me how much I love to suck on your—"

"*Trey.* We're still in the hallway, in case you hadn't noticed."

"I noticed, all right. Pick up the pace a little, will you, Masterson?"

"I'm walking as fast as I can in these shoes."

"I can see that. Did you know that walking fast in those things makes you jiggle? That's a bonus."

She stared at him. She'd never seen him quite like this. "Have you been drinking?"

"Not yet, but I plan to. I should have had you take the shoes off, except I have an image of doing you when you're wearing them."

"Trey, you're out of control." And she loved it.

"Sweetheart, you have no idea. How easy does that slinky number come off, anyway?"

"It just pulls over my head."

"Excellent. Once we're in the room, put down the plates and take it off. I'll handle things from there."

"So we'll have wild monkey sex and then walk back into the party like nothing happened?"

He glanced at her. "You have a problem with that?"

"Not at all."

12

If Elle had offered any protest, Trey would have dialed back his enthusiasm. But she was on board with the program, which gave him another dose of confidence for the future. Elle liked being a little wild, and that's why they were perfect for each other.

At the door to his room, he had to set down both champagne flutes while he dug out his key. But he got the door open, picked up the flutes, and followed Elle inside. The room looked pristine, because he'd let the maid have her way in here.

That had killed him, because he'd liked the rumpled sheets that still carried the scent of sex and Elle. But he'd picked up on Elle's desire for order, something she'd probably learned from her military parents. He could be orderly when it was important.

But she didn't seem to notice the crisp look of the room. Following his directions, she set both plates on his desk and pulled her knit dress over her head. The effect of Elle standing there in a skimpy bra, lacy panties and silver heels… He nearly dropped both champagne flutes.

She gazed at him. "Isn't this what you wanted?"

"Oh, yeah." He propped his butt against the door and pulled off his boots. "Don't move. Let me look at you while I get out of my boots and jeans."

"And your shirt." Her mouth tilted up at the corners. "You'll be up on the stage pretty soon. I don't want you looking as if you just had a roll in the hay."

"Why not?" But after he shucked his jeans and briefs, he took off his shirt, too. "Rock stars do it all the time."

"Is that what we're about to have? Rock star sex?"

"I have no idea what that is." He tossed the condom he'd carried in his jeans pocket as insurance—he'd had no idea whether she'd be up for this when he got dressed—onto the desk. Then he closed the distance between them and wrapped her warm body in his arms. "But any rock star in the world would be lucky to find you in his room between sets."

"Flatterer." She lifted her mouth to his.

"Nope." He leaned down and took a small taste, which required control because he felt like a starving man at a feast. "You're the real deal, Elle. You're incredibly beautiful without being a diva. You're fiery in bed, but I have the feeling that's a well-kept secret."

She wrapped her arms around him. "Very well kept. Only two people know it."

He groaned and rested his forehead against hers. "Do you realize how important that is? Dear God, Elle. You and I have opened ourselves to each other in ways that some people never do."

She heaved a breath. "Is this going to be a deep discussion? Because I don't think we have time for that before the next set."

"You're right." And he was officially an idiot, which came as no surprise. "We have time for one spectacular climax each, and then we have to go back to the reception."

"I'm still wearing the silver stilettos."

"So you are." He hooked his thumbs in the elastic of her delicate panties and drew them down over her incredible legs until he reached the floor. "Step out, please."

She did, with grace and style.

He tossed the panties over his shoulder and stood. "Rock star sex seems as if it should be up against a hard surface." He scooped up the condom and handed it to her. "Keep track of that for me."

"I don't think a rock star would make his date hold his condom."

"Maybe not, but I'm new at this." Catching her around the waist, he swung her up and around until she was braced against the door.

"The door? Really?"

"It has multiple advantages. While we're getting it on, nobody can force their way in."

"Is that likely?"

"You never know. Condom, please?"

She started laughing. "I feel like a character in a dark comedy." But she handed him the condom.

He desperately needed it for his aching cock, which was in danger of detonating before its time. She might think this was some sort of comedy, but seeing her clothed in nothing but a push-up bra and stilettos was playing havoc with his restraint.

He rolled on the condom and grasped her hips. His gaze traveled down to the silver straps and impossible high heels, and he wondered if he was into kinky, because seeing those things made his balls tighten painfully. "Wrap your legs around me and hold on to my shoulders."

"Now I feel like a performer in Cirque du Soleil."

He blew out a breath. "Just do it."

She did, and despite her smart-ass comments, her breathing was jerky and uneven. She might be into this as much as he was. When he looked into her eyes, he was certain of it. Blue flames danced there.

Her silver heels pressed against the small of his back, which made him aware of them, even though they were out of sight. He liked that. Yeah, he might be a little kinky.

Once he had her positioned properly, with her back firmly against the door, he eased forward, seeking that slick channel he knew awaited him. He wasn't disappointed. Judging by how wet she was, she'd been as impatient for this moment as he'd been.

Her breath caught. "I've never done it up against a door."

"Me, either, but I think I like it." He locked in tight and met her gaze. *Yes.* "Can you balance and unfasten your bra?"

"Why?"

"I want to watch your breasts quiver when I push into you."

"You're crazy."

"I want it all, Elle. Every bit of this."

Sucking in a breath, she let go of his shoulders long enough to flip open the front closure of her bra. The material fell away, revealing creamy skin and nipples tight with desire.

"Yeah. Like that." He drew back and rocked forward. Her body shook from the impact, giving him exactly the visual he'd been hoping for.

She moaned.

"Is that a good moan or a bad moan?"

She licked her lips. "A good moan. Do that again."

"With pleasure." He slid back, but not too far, and drove home once more.

"That's...nice." Her gaze lost focus, as if her concentration had shifted, moved to that locus of all things wonderful.

"Want more?"

"Yes. Please."

Sure of the territory now, he initiated a slow rhythm. She gripped his shoulders and met each thrust as they created a steady thumping noise against the door. At first he worried about that. But as the tension grew, he gave up worrying, closed his eyes and let himself feel—the delicious friction, the liquid heat, the surge of adrenaline when she tightened around his cock, signaling... Oh, yeah, she was coming, and so was he, in a furious rush of pleasure. She gasped and cried out. He shoved deep and stayed there, his cock pulsing, his brain spinning, his spirit soaring. *So. Good.*

He opened his eyes. The sight of her leaning back against the door, her gaze open and vulnerable, touched something so deep within his heart that he'd never forget this moment. Any second now she could pull up the drawbridge and lock him out.

But if she'd dared to leave the door open, then he would dare the perilous walk through it. "I'm falling in love with you, Elle."

For one shining moment, joy filled her expression. Then, as if she'd pushed a switch, the light dimmed. "It's too soon," she said gently. She touched his face with a trembling hand. "You were half in love with me before we met. You're falling for the idea of me."

His jaw tightened. "No, I'm falling for you, Elle Masterson."

"It's the sex."

"Of course it's the sex! And because we've had so damned much of it, I've found out you're warm, and giving, and funny, and adventuresome, and bawdy and incredibly…real."

She swallowed. "You are such a romantic. You're so good with words. You know exactly what to say to make it seem as if—"

"Damn it, don't dismiss what I've said because you've got it in your head that I'm some sort of crazy dreamer who's out of touch with reality."

"Trey, you are a dreamer."

"Okay, I'll own that label. But because I'm a dreamer, I pick up on things that other people might not. I *know* you, Elle. Every time we've been together, I've soaked that knowledge in through my pores. But do you know me? At all?"

Her expression closed down. "Maybe not. And we should go."

"Yes, we should." He wouldn't get anywhere with her now, anyway. She was blocking him, blocking the truth because it scared the devil out of her. She couldn't make the leap with him, at least not yet.

Easing away from her, he supported her until she was standing again. Then he turned and walked into the bathroom. She was right about one thing. It was too soon, but not for him. It was too soon for her.

She was right about something else, too. He had been half in love with her before they met, and for a very good reason. By rescuing him, she'd shown that she was brave and caring. He'd felt it in her touch. He'd recognized it in her determination to get him to safety.

And most of all, he'd heard the warmth in her voice. He'd fallen in love with the sound. Maybe he hadn't consciously analyzed why, but he could do that now. He was good with auditory cues, and her voice had been filled with compassion.

During that crisis, the soul of Elle Masterson had come shining through. She hadn't been cautious and logical when she'd come upon him in the snow. If she had been, she would have called 911. Instead, unwilling to depend on others when every second counted, she'd acted.

That was the woman he was falling in love with. Correction—he'd already fallen, but he'd decided to frame it differently so he wouldn't scare her so much. He'd scared her, anyway. Next time he'd give her the unvarnished truth.

And there would be a next time, he vowed as he walked back into the room. She was already dressed. She peered into the mirror over the desk while she tucked strands of blond hair back into the arrangement on top of her head.

"I like your hair like that."

She took a rhinestone hairpin out of her mouth and fastened it in place. "Thanks."

"Elle, I don't want to fight with you."

She turned toward him, her expression cautious. "I don't want to fight with you, either. I like you a lot."

He supposed that was something. "So you'll come back here with me after the party?"

"I'm afraid you'll get hurt."

He grabbed his clothes and started putting them on. "Look, if you're worried that I'll slip a disk, we can forget about the weird positions tonight. I admit that up against the door put a strain on my back."

"I meant—"

"No, really." He dressed quickly. "Missionary works fine for me. Or you can be on top, which is really easy on my spine."

She smiled and shook her head. "Okay, we won't talk about it."

"Good. Actions speak louder than words, anyway." He checked the time on his phone. "Wow, we were amazingly fast. Alex should have things under control for another ten minutes, at least."

"Then you should eat."

"I do believe I will. And drink." He crossed to the desk and picked up one of the champagne flutes. "Here's to great sex."

She glanced at him, as if wondering what he was up to. But she took her flute and touched it to his. "To great sex."

Elle tasted her champagne. "Wow. Nice."

"That's Pam Mulholland for you. She likes to go first-class, although I think she realized that caviar would be wasted on this bunch."

"Is she Pam Sterling now?"

"You know, I don't think so. I seem to remember hearing that she decided she'd keep her name, and

Emmett was fine with that." He picked up one of the miniature quiches and took a bite.

"Really? That's interesting."

"They're not going to be the typical couple living in a cottage with a white picket fence. Pam will stay at her B and B as usual, and Emmett will keep his little house at the ranch. They've been spending the night together off and on for years. Nothing much will change in their lifestyle." He gestured toward the plates. "You should eat one of these little sandwiches. They're amazing." He popped the rest of his into his mouth.

"So why get married?" Elle picked up a sandwich.

"Good question. From what I hear, Pam wanted to make what had been a private arrangement more public." He laughed. "And she wanted a party. I think a good part of it was staging this extravaganza. She runs a B and B for a reason. She's a very social person."

"Is Emmett?" Elle still hadn't taken a bite of her sandwich.

"Not as much as she is, but after today, I'll bet he gets into it more. They'll be good for each other." He glanced at the sandwich in her hand. "You'd better eat. We should leave pretty soon and this stuff will be trashed by the time we get back."

"Oh." She looked at the sandwich as if she'd forgotten all about it. "You're right." She ate it and reached for another.

"The veggies are good, too." He bit into a carrot stick.

She laughed.

"What?" He liked hearing her laugh, but he didn't know why she had.

"You sound like my mother. *Eat your veggies. They're good for you.*"

"Well, they are, but I damn sure don't want to be mistaken for your mother. I do, however, think you need to keep up your strength for later." He waggled his eyebrows as he popped a cherry tomato in his mouth.

The eyebrow routine made her laugh, too. "I'm sure you're right, but that's all I have time for." She drained her champagne flute and set it on the desk. "I need a couple of minutes to fix my makeup before we go back out there."

"That sounds like my cue to grab a kiss before you start doing that." He put down his glass.

"We're liable to be late."

"We won't be late."

"I don't know about this."

"It'll be fine." He drew her into his arms.

She flattened her hands against his chest. "Trey, you know what happens when you kiss me. I lose all sense of time."

"Not me. I'm a human stopwatch. We have thirty seconds on the clock. Go." He swooped in.

She was laughing when he connected with her mouth, so he had easy access for his tongue. He used it wisely, letting her know what they'd be doing after the party tonight. He cupped her head with care, not wanting to disturb the arrangement she'd fixed moments ago.

But he held her firmly, not allowing her to pull away, because he wanted to give her a kiss that would last for a couple of hours, at least. For the first few seconds, she refused to yield to temptation, but as the kiss heated up, she wrapped her arms around his neck and settled against him.

He deepened the kiss, and she moaned. Good. He wanted to leave her with a moaning kind of kiss. He wanted to leave her with a heavy breathing kind of kiss, too, and they were accomplishing that goal.

To finish, he pulled her in tight so she could feel his erection pressing against her belly. He wanted to leave her with that information, too, in case she needed reminding that while he was playing his guitar, he'd be thinking of what they'd be doing once they came back to his room.

Although he had no idea whether thirty seconds had gone by or not, he lifted his head and started to let her go. She wanted to fix her makeup, and only a selfish jerk would use up all her time so she couldn't do that. With a murmur of protest, she pulled his head down and kept kissing.

O-kay. He wasn't going to argue with that. If she was hungrier for his kiss than for that sandwich, so be it. His state of arousal increased exponentially. He massaged her cute little fanny through her skirt, and somehow it rode up, and now he was touching silk.

Not long afterward, he was stroking bare skin as she writhed against him. Then, with a groan of frustration, she wiggled out of his arms. She was panting. "See what I mean?" She pulled up her panties and smoothed down her dress.

"I do." He was secretly so happy that he wanted to punch his fist in the air, but he controlled himself. A victory dance right now would be in poor taste. He also wanted to ask her about Argentina again. He didn't do that, either. But if she thought she could leave this kind of passion and jet off to Argentina, she had another think coming.

13

ELLE REALIZED HER behavior was erratic, which was not like her. As she walked back to the party holding Trey's hand, the term *temporary insanity* flitted through her mind. She'd never met a man this compelling.

Although she'd had fun with those other guys she'd dated, they hadn't affected her as Trey did. He'd asked if she knew him at all, and she'd lied. From that first moment in his arms, she'd felt as if she'd known him forever.

But that feeling of connection had to be a result of sexual chemistry, right? She couldn't have bonded with him on any other level, not in the short time they'd spent together. And yet, being with him felt so right. They interacted with a kind of ease that should take much longer to develop.

Trey's attitude had a lot to do with that. He'd treated her as a good friend from the beginning, because after the rescue, he'd thought of her that way. His assumption that they belonged together was hard to resist.

She would resist it, though. Facts were facts. His

life as a ranch hand didn't mesh well with her life as a ski instructor. Her present career path spanned two continents. He might be willing to brush that barrier aside, but she wasn't. She hadn't known him long enough to justify rearranging her life.

Alex was still spinning tunes when they walked in, and Trey pulled Elle onto the dance floor. "One number."

"It's country swing. I'm not that familiar with—" But she laughed and gave in, because Trey wasn't going to take no for an answer.

Besides, only a person with no rhythm at all would have trouble dancing with Trey. His sense of the music traveled through his arms and his fingertips as he guided her through the movements. Soon she was twirling and two-stepping like a pro.

He grinned at her as she spun under his arm. "You're a natural."

"No, you're a fantastic partner."

"I'll take that, especially if it's a global statement."

"Global?"

"Covering all partner-type activities."

"I have no idea what you're talking about."

"Yes, you do. You're blushing."

She'd believe it. Between the fast dance and the sex they'd just had, she might have acquired a permanent blush.

When the music ended, Alex announced that the live music makers were back in the house. Trey planted a firm kiss on Elle's mouth before hopping up on the stage. Watkins followed at a slower pace.

Mary Lou walked up beside her. "We looked for you two during the break, but you disappeared."

Elle wondered if her cheeks could possibly get any hotter. "Oh. We, um, decided to—"

"That's okay, honey." Mary Lou patted her arm. "I was young once. In fact, even now, Watkins likes to be spontaneous, if you know what I mean." She winked. "And judging from your expression, I'm sure you do."

Elle struggled to think of a response.

"You look thirsty," Mary Lou said. "What do you say we get some champagne and sit for a minute?"

"Good idea." Elle didn't have a better one. She chose not to point out that champagne wouldn't quench a person's thirst. She suspected Mary Lou knew that.

Moments later they found a spot at a little table and sat down with their champagne.

"This is the good stuff," Mary Lou said. "Never pass up a chance to drink expensive champagne. That's my motto." She took a sip.

Elle swallowed a mouthful, and the bubbles tickled her tongue. "I think I'll adopt that motto, too."

"You're welcome to it. So, when are you coming out to the ranch?"

"I don't know."

"Now would be a great time, when there's plenty of room. In the summer the boys arrive, and then things are more hectic. Oh, I forgot. You might not know what I mean about those boys."

"I do, actually." Elle discovered that good champagne went down easily. "I looked up the ranch on the internet last night. It sounds like a great program."

"It is. You'd get a kick out of those boys. But you said you'd be in Argentina all summer." Mary Lou finished her champagne. "These glasses are pretty, but they don't hold much. Want a refill?"

Elle hesitated.

"Ah, come on. You're not driving anywhere. And remember the motto."

"Never pass up a chance to drink expensive champagne." Elle held out her empty flute. "Fill 'er up, Mary Lou."

"That's the ticket."

While she was off getting them more bubbly, Elle redirected her attention to the bandstand. Trey and Tyler were singing the country standard "Jackson," which was funny considering that the song was about Jackson, Mississippi, yet they had a town of Jackson right down the road. The two obviously had fun with the lyrics, as each taunted the other about making a splash in Jackson now that their love affair had burned itself out.

"That's real cute, isn't it?" Mary Lou set a full glass in front of Elle. "I've seen them perform that one before, and it's a crowd pleaser, since we have a Jackson right next door."

"They do a great job." Elle couldn't help paying attention to the lyrics, though, which described the danger of hooking up with someone because of hot sex, which in the case of the Johnny Cash song, faded fast.

When Trey and Tyler finished, she clapped and cheered like everyone else. But she continued to think about those lyrics. She turned to Mary Lou. "How long did you know Watkins before you married him?"

"A long time. I'll bet I've known him almost twenty years. And he was after me the minute he set foot on the ranch."

"He was?" Elle realized that sounded rude. "I mean, of course he was. You're—"

"Hey, it's okay. I'm gray and plump now, but twenty years ago, I could stop traffic. Well, that's not hard to do in Shoshone. We don't have much traffic and only the one light at the intersection."

Elle was fascinated. And slightly smashed. "So he wanted you, but you didn't agree to marry him for almost twenty years?"

"I didn't want to marry anyone, including Watkins. My plumbing's wonky and I couldn't have kids, so why get married? Besides, I liked being single."

"So do I." It was the answer she always gave, but she felt a twinge of resistance this time. Entirely Trey's fault, too.

"I pegged you for an independent woman from the get-go." She took another sip of her champagne. "Want some munchies? I could go for some munchies."

"Sure, why not?" If she intended to continue drinking champagne with Mary Lou, she needed more food in her stomach. The conversation was just getting interesting, though, so she wanted a reason to keep sitting there.

Mary Lou returned with plates of various kinds of cheese and more of the petits fours, plus a mountain of chocolate-dipped strawberries, which were a real luxury in December. "I'm in the mood to indulge," she said.

"So am I." Elle picked up a strawberry and took a bite. Champagne went great with chocolate-covered strawberries. "So after holding out against matrimony all those years, what changed your mind?"

"Watkins was pitiful."

Elle choked on her champagne.

"Easy, girl." Mary Lou patted her on the back.

"Didn't know you had a mouthful of champagne or I would have waited until you swallowed."

Elle dragged in a breath. "I'm fine. So you married Watkins because you felt sorry for him?"

"No, that's not right. I married him because he loved me more than life itself. And when I climbed down off my high horse and thought about it, I realized I'd loved him all that time, too. I'm not sorry I waited. Made him appreciate me more."

"I'll bet it did." Elle lifted her glass in Mary Lou's direction. "A toast to holding out."

"It has its advantages." Mary Lou finished her second glass. "One more?"

"Okay, but this is it. Someone will have to carry me out of here if I have more than that."

"I know someone who would volunteer for the job."

"So do I."

Mary Lou smiled. "Be right back. Don't go away. I have a point I want to make."

"You've already made a few, and I appreciate them all." Elle basked in the rosy glow of expensive champagne and the knowledge that Trey wanted her as desperately as Watkins had wanted Mary Lou.

But then there was that pesky Johnny Cash song to be considered. If Elle gave in, would the fire burn out? She ate another strawberry as she thought about that.

"Here we go." Mary Lou set a brimming champagne flute in front of Elle. "That bartender is a sweetheart."

"Amy? She is. I should go over and say hi. In fact, I should probably help her behind the bar."

"Not tonight. You're a guest, and from the looks of her tip jar, Amy will do very well tonight. The booze may be free, but the Last Chance folks are good tip-pers."

"I don't doubt it. There's an almost noble quality in the website. I get the feeling it's very good to be connected to the Last Chance Ranch. They're highly thought of in the area."

"They are, and I love working there. Which brings me to my point." She took time to drink more champagne.

"Mary Lou, I don't think I've ever had better champagne than this. Thank you for inviting me to sit and share a glass…or several."

"I had the feeling we might have some things in common. I get the sense you don't think finding a man is the Holy Grail, either."

"Hell, no." Elle clapped a hand over her mouth. "Whoops. I probably shouldn't be swearing in the middle of a wedding reception."

Mary Lou waved a dismissive hand. "Don't worry about it. These are ranch folks. They're used to swearing. But back to the point I wanted to make."

"Which is?" Elle took another swallow of this most excellent champagne.

"The whole time I was holding Watkins off, and let me add that during that time we had some sexy interludes, I was living right where he was living. He had to see me every day, and vice versa."

"That was convenient, but if you're comparing your situation to mine, I work as a ski instructor. In order to do that in the summer, I have to go to the opposite side of the equator."

Mary Lou nodded and swallowed more champagne. "That's fine, but I don't know if you can hold Trey off *and* spend six months in Argentina. If he doesn't see you all the time…"

"But if we're meant for each other, shouldn't he be fine with the separation?"

"In a perfect world, yes. But this is a man we're talking about. He'll get testy. You'll quarrel. It won't go well."

"Then I guess it won't work out." Elle felt a sharp pain in the region of her heart.

"Are you sure that's what you want? To have everything fall apart? Isn't there some work you could do in Jackson Hole for the summer?"

Elle gazed at Mary Lou. "How would that look? I change my entire schedule so I can hang around here and wait tables? Talk about pathetic."

"I see what you mean. I don't picture you turning into a groupie, Elle. You're better than that."

"Thank you! Finally somebody understands my position."

"But I also see the way Trey looks at you. He's as smitten as Watkins ever was." She leaned closer. "Woman to woman, that kind of devotion can be fabulous."

"So what should I do?"

Mary Lou shrugged. "Drink more champagne."

WHENEVER TREY GLANCED over at the table where Elle sat with Mary Lou, they had their heads together, and they seemed to be thoroughly enjoying each other and the champagne. Trey figured having Mary Lou and Elle buddy up could go one of two ways. Mary Lou might try to sell her on the idea of ranches and cowboys, or she might encourage Elle's independent spirit, which logically meant heading off to Argentina in April as planned.

In the end, Elle would do what she wanted, though. He just hoped that what she wanted turned out to be the same thing he did—for them to be together. Still, he couldn't help wondering what had transpired between the two women while he'd been stuck behind a microphone.

Mary Lou was a staunch feminist and Trey admired that. He'd never thought women should defer to men. Mary Lou and Watkins were a volatile combination, but they were devoted to each other. Come to think of it, Mary Lou and Elle had a lot of traits in common. No wonder they'd hit it off.

The party took a long time to wind down. Pam and Emmett left, but no one else seemed ready to give up. Tomorrow was a free day, with nothing on the schedule except a morning ski lesson and the after-lunch send-off for Pam and Emmett.

Pam had hired a limo to take them to the airport for their flight to Tahiti. Trey laughed every time he thought of Emmett lounging on a beach with an umbrella drink in his hand. He'd return a changed man.

Pam and Emmett's love story had come to a happy ending. Trey wasn't convinced that his and Elle's love story was bound for the same kind of bliss. They had many unresolved issues. Although he wished they could resolve them in bed, he doubted that would happen.

Even so, he was willing to try. The sooner this party ended, the sooner he could hustle Elle back to his room and continue to show her why they were meant for each other. But this was turning into the never-ending celebration.

Sometime around one in the morning, when Trey's fingers had grown numb from playing, Alex became his favorite human being of all time, excluding Elle, of course.

"You guys have gone above and beyond," Alex said. "This group isn't ready to quit, and it takes less energy for me to spin tunes than for you to play. Give it up."

"I appreciate that," Watkins said. "Years ago I could have plucked this guitar 'til dawn, but those days are gone."

"Nobody should play until dawn," Alex said. "I'll close the place down in another hour or so, but I give both of you permission to vamoose, along with the companion of your choice."

Watkins chuckled. "That sounds great. Come on, Trey. Let's go get our women."

"Amen to that." Trey was glad Elle wasn't there to hear Watkins's somewhat chauvinistic comment. Mary Lou would have given him hell for it, too. Neither of those ladies would consider themselves some man's *woman*.

Watkins knew that, but sometimes he liked to talk like the good ol' boy he'd been raised to be. He'd been around Mary Lou long enough to know when he could get away with it and when he couldn't.

Judging from the happy expressions worn by both Elle and Mary Lou, the men wouldn't have to worry too much about being politically correct tonight. Pam's champagne and good conversation had worked its magic and they were all smiles.

"I see you both have your guitars," Mary Lou said. "Does that mean you're finished for the night?"

Watkins nodded and sank into a chair next to Mary Lou. "Alex took pity on us."

"Want some champagne?" Mary Lou handed him her glass, which was half-full.

"Don't mind if I do." He polished it off.

Mary Lou motioned to Trey, who'd remained standing. "Take a load off, cowboy. There's plenty of champagne left. Pam ordered an ungodly amount of this stuff."

"And Mary Lou has taught me her motto," Elle said. "Never pass up a chance to drink expensive champagne."

Trey gazed at her. She was adorable. And slightly sloshed. "Thanks, but I'm ready to call it a night. You three can have my share." He wouldn't assume she'd want to go back with him. He hoped, but he wouldn't assume.

"You know, I've had enough champagne, too." Elle pushed back her chair, picked up her silver purse and stood.

He smiled at her. "Then I'll walk you home."

"That would be lovely."

Watkins laughed. "You two behave yourselves, okay?"

"Pay no attention to him," Mary Lou said. "Go have fun."

"Thanks, Mary Lou." Trey tucked his arm around Elle's waist, and his world clicked into focus again. "We will." He'd been aching to hold her for hours. The time had come.

14

ELLE MOVED DOWN the hallway in a sensual daze. She was desired by a sexy man who turned her on. She had reservations about the future, but none about the present. After consuming a fairly large quantity of champagne, she was ready to live in the present, at least for the next twenty-four hours.

But instead of guiding her through the lobby and down to his room, Trey was heading up the stairs in the direction of her room. She glanced at him. "Where are we going?"

"I have a plan, if you're willing to go along with it. How about packing up whatever you need for tonight and tomorrow morning and bringing it to my room?"

"You want me to stay in your room all night?"

"That's the idea."

She smiled. "I like it."

"I was hoping you would."

She climbed the stairs and wished they'd taken the elevator. She'd had enough of walking in these heels. "I can ditch these shoes while I'm at it."

"Uh, for now, sure, but I was hoping that you'd put them on later, when we—"

"Trey Wheeler, you are a wicked boy." Thoughts of stretching out in his bed wearing only her shoes sent a jolt of lust to all the places he'd soon be paying close attention to.

"Will you do it?"

"As long as I don't have to walk all the way back to your room in them."

"You can walk to my room barefoot and wearing a bathrobe for all I care. In fact, why not?"

"Sorry, cowboy. I'm not parading through the lobby in a bathrobe. It's one thing for the entire place to know we're having sex. It's quite another to flaunt the fact."

"Do we have to go through the lobby? Isn't there a service elevator we could use?"

She hadn't thought of that. She seldom took the regular elevator, let alone the service one. But the cleaning and maintenance staff wouldn't be using it tonight, now would they?

As she pictured herself riding the service elevator to the main floor, which would bypass the lobby, another image came to mind. She'd never had elevator sex. Either she was very inspired by Trey or very tipsy on champagne. Maybe both. Ordinarily she wouldn't consider such a thing.

"I'll change into my bathrobe and we'll take the service elevator." She grew damp thinking about what she had in mind. The concept seemed clandestine and daring. No one would come along, but someone *could,* which made the sex more exciting.

They reached her door, and she was ready with

the key. Now that elevator sex was on the docket, her adrenaline level had shot up. He might not go along with the idea, but she had a feeling he might. For this she might leave on the shoes.

Earlier today she'd scrounged an extension cord so that her Christmas tree was connected to the plug activated by the switch next to her door. That way she could turn on the tree whenever she walked in instead of using her bedside lamp. She'd become fond of the glow.

Trey followed her into the room. "Pretty little tree."

"Thanks." She grabbed a small duffel bag and threw some underwear and her ski clothes into it, along with her room key. Then she took some toiletries out of the bathroom and tossed those in, too.

"I thought you weren't into Christmas."

"I'm not really, but they give the employees trees every year, so it seems a waste not to decorate them." She took the pins out of her hair and laid them on her dresser before pulling her dress over her head and hanging it up in the closet.

"You look good in Christmas light."

She turned. The soft colors from the tree bathed him in a rosy hue that made her think of a fantasy cowboy. "So do you."

"Now I wish I had a Christmas tree in my room, so I could make love to you in this light."

"But you have that big ol' bed and I don't." She unfastened her bra and stepped out of her panties, but left on the shoes.

"God, you're beautiful."

"It's the light." She pulled her fluffy white bathrobe off its hanger.

"It's way more than the light, but those colors reflected on your skin are amazing." He glanced at the bathrobe in her hand. "Don't put that on yet. Give me a minute to look at you."

"Trey, I feel silly just standing here."

"You're not silly. You're a goddess. I've always been so intent on the sex that I haven't stopped to admire you. Humor me."

She let out a sigh of surrender. "Good thing I've had all that champagne or I'd be even more self-conscious." As long as he was going to study her, she might as well give him her best pose. Shoulders back, breasts out, stomach in.

"Wow."

Okay. Now that she'd gotten past the first few seconds of this, she realized that posing for him was turning her on. She was aware of his gaze traveling over every inch of her body, and she grew warm and achy as he continued to look.

His low chuckle sounded sexy and intimate. "Are you liking this better now?"

"Why do you ask?"

"Your breathing has changed and your nipples are erect."

"Maybe I'm cold."

"Or maybe you're hot." He drew in a ragged breath. "But even if you're not, I sure am. Either we leave or we make use of your little twin bed."

"Are you prepared for that?"

"Sweetheart, I've been prepared since that first night with you. I never leave home without those little raincoats. So which will it be? Stay or leave?"

"Leave." When she put on her bathrobe, the soft

terry made her skin tingle. She tied the belt and picked up her duffel bag. Walking reminded her of how damp her thighs were. "Let's go."

"Weren't you planning to take off those shoes?"

"Eventually. I'll leave them on a little longer."

"I won't argue with you on that. Watching you strut around in those shoes and knowing you have nothing on under your robe will be all the foreplay I'll need between here and my room."

She smiled as she thought about what would happen between here and his room. Up to now, he'd been the one with all the ideas. She would show him that she had a few of her own.

She directed him through another set of double doors on the second floor, and they were once more in the guest area. Fortunately, the hallway was empty. She'd rather not encounter anyone on their way to the elevator. After they reached it, they'd be fine. It opened not far from his room on the first floor.

"If anyone comes along, we're heading for the pool," she said.

"This place has a pool?"

"It's set up as an indoor pool this time of year, but in the summer, the glass canopy slides back. Or so I'm told. I'm never here then, so I haven't seen it that way."

"If this is primarily a ski lodge, what goes on in the summer?"

"Hiking, mountain biking, swimming, fishing. Serenity has tennis courts. There's an arrangement with one of the local stables if people want to ride."

"A bunch of summer sports, then."

"Exactly. But I don't do summer sports."

"Why not?"

She glanced at him. She knew why he was asking. Obviously there were jobs here in the summer for those who were into those things. "I love the challenge of skiing. I love the thrill of it. And I've put a lot of time into learning how to do it well. The summer activities seem tame by comparison."

"Makes sense." He was silent for a moment. "What about hang gliding?"

She couldn't help laughing. "Since I've never done it, I doubt I could get a job teaching it."

"Not right away, but I just—"

"You'd like me to find a summer job here."

"I would. I realize that's a lot to ask, but the plain fact is I wish you didn't have to leave in April."

"I know." She doubted that he really wanted to have this discussion now. She certainly didn't. "I don't know what the future holds for us, but…could we not talk about that tonight?"

His quick glance told her he realized they might be veering into difficult territory. "You're right. This is not the time or the place." His smile returned. "Or the outfit. A guy would have to be pretty dumb to talk about serious things when a woman is wearing shoes like yours."

She let out her breath in relief. "You like these shoes, huh?"

"Love 'em."

"Good. And look at that. Here's the service elevator."

"So it is. We're making progress." He stepped forward and pushed the button.

A current of excitement ran through her body, setting off little tremors of anticipation. He had no idea, poor man, but she was about to blow his mind. The doors rumbled open to reveal a spacious, utilitarian interior. Bright lights illuminated bare walls and no handrails. It was a stark cube, and all the more exotic to her because of that.

Trey gestured her forward. "After you."

She'd thought about her presentation ever since the idea had come to her. Sashaying into the elevator, she dropped her duffel to the floor and turned around to face him. As he stepped in and the doors began to close behind him, she untied her robe. Opening the lapels, she flashed him.

His gasp echoed off the walls. "What the hell are you doing?"

"Hit the stop button, cowboy. Then unzip and come on over here. I have something for you."

He whirled and smacked the stop button, but then he slowly turned back to her. "Are you serious?"

"Would I kid about something like this?" She cupped her breasts and fondled her nipples. That moment when he'd stared at her in the room had made her bolder. "See what a little champagne can do to my inhibitions?"

His set his guitar case down. "And I thought all we'd get was an elevator ride." He sounded short of breath.

"I have a different ride in mind." She slid one hand between her legs. "Care to mount up?"

Unfastening his belt and unzipping his jeans, he came toward her. "I'm going to find out what brand of champagne that was and order a case of it."

She licked her lips. "I did enjoy the bubbly."

"And now I'm going to enjoy you." Pulling a condom out of his pocket, he handed it to her. "Since this is your party, I'll let you do the honors."

"Be glad to." She ripped open the foil.

He planted one hand on either side of her head, caging her in as he leaned forward. "Put it on tight. This could get wild." Then he began playing with her mouth as he told her in great detail what he was about to do to her. After sucking on her lower lip, he used several four-letter words to paint a picture of his intentions. He ran his tongue over the bow of her upper lip and continued the litany of earthy predictions. He nibbled and promised. He lapped and suggested.

By the time she'd rolled the condom on, she was frantic to have him. Her breasts quivered with each breath. "You're ready."

"Oh, yeah. I'm so ready." He hooked his arm under the back of her knee. Leaving one hand braced against the wall beside her head, he raised her leg, probed her slick heat and pushed inside, groaning with satisfaction.

She was pinned to the elevator wall by his cock, and she loved it. He felt so damned good there—right there. "What was it you said you were going to do to me?"

"Lady, I'm doing it." He drew back and thrust forward again with firm deliberation. His hot gaze bored into her. "And I intend to keep doing it until you beg for mercy." He shoved in tighter, pushing her back against the wall. "I feel as if I could climb right inside you."

Her heart beat wildly. "Go ahead."

"Believe I will." He began to move, and each

stroke drove deep, touching her core, ratcheting up the tension.

She gasped with pleasure.

"Like that?" His eyes sparked fire.

She stared right back at him, unflinching. "Yes. Bring it on."

His breath caught. "Oh, Elle." With a noise that was nearly a growl, he surged forward, pounding into her without pause. The liquid sound of his cock driving into her created an echo that made the tiny cubicle resonate with passion.

Delirious with the untamed force of his body entering hers over and over, Elle surrendered to her orgasm with panting cries of delight. He kept going, and she came again, breathless with wonder.

"Now," he muttered. *"Now."* And he shoved her back against the wall one more time. As his cock pulsed within her, he lowered his head, and his gasps were punctuated with several colorful swear words.

Long seconds later, he lifted his head and looked into her eyes. A smile twitched at the corners of his mouth. "You continue to surprise the hell out of me."

"Glad to hear it."

"That was outstanding."

"I thought so. That's the first time you swore while you were coming."

He chuckled and shook his head. "Guess I did. I was out of my mind." He glanced around at the elevator. "I think it was partly the acoustics."

"The *acoustics?*"

"Yeah. The way the sounds bounced around in here seemed to amplify the sensation, sort of like a sex rock concert."

"Oh, my God." She started to laugh. "So this is what it's like to have sex with a musician. They're into how it sounds."

"Of course." He looked surprised that she hadn't figured that out. "I love the sound of sex. There's the moaning, the fast breathing, the lapping, the sucking, the incredibly erotic noise of my cock slipping in and out of your—"

"I get it." And her body wanted it again. The stirrings were unmistakable. "But we need to untangle ourselves. I'm losing feeling in my leg."

"Can't have that."

Putting everything to rights again took some doing, but they eventually managed. Fortunately, Trey was the kind of old-fashioned guy who carried a handkerchief in his back pocket. He said usually he carried a bandanna. The handkerchief was for special occasions like weddings.

"And having sex in service elevators?" Elle winked at him.

"Apparently so. I'll add it to my list of must-haves whenever I'm with you. Gotta make sure I have at least one condom and a handkerchief. Then we can do it anywhere."

"What a concept."

He gazed at her. "I know. Now I'm wondering what other places have interesting acoustics."

"So we're back to the acoustics?"

"Well, *yeah*." He pushed the button and the elevator started back down. "Creaky beds are good. I'd love to find a set of those old-fashioned springs. A creaky old bed with metal springs, inside a small room with tile floors and no curtains, would give you a sexual symphony. I'd love to try that."

"Sounds loud."

"It would be loud, and wild. Then add in your voice saying naughty words in that husky way you have, and your moans, and little cries…" He reached out and ran a finger down her cheek. "I hope you're not sleepy yet."

"Please don't say we're going out in search of a tiled room with a squeaky bed."

"Not tonight. But even a cushy king-size mattress is capable of very nice sounds when two people are making love on it."

She realized that he'd switched the terminology from having sex to making love. Judging from the warm light in his brown eyes, he'd done it on purpose. They'd had plenty of wild sex. She suspected the next round would be about something else entirely. She might not be ready for that.

15

CREATIVE SEXUAL EXPERIENCES were all well and good, Trey thought as he opened the door to his room and ushered Elle inside. But tenderness was important, too, and they hadn't shared enough of that. He wasn't complaining. He'd remember that elevator ride for the rest of his life.

Time to dial back the frenzy, though, and show her a different kind of loving—his favorite kind. She walked in on those crazy shoes, and he decided those would be the first to go. He was responsible for her keeping them on, because he'd relished the fantasy of a woman wearing do-me shoes and nothing else.

He didn't need that anymore. They'd had that brand of fantasy sex in the elevator. He closed and locked the door before turning back to her. "You can take off your shoes if you want to."

Her blue eyes flashed with a hint of an emotion he couldn't identify. "You're sure?"

"I'm sure. In fact, sit on the bed and let me take them off for you."

She chuckled as she perched on the edge of the mattress. "Oh, I know where this is going."

"Do you?" He didn't think so. He sat cross-legged on the floor in front of her and took one foot into his lap. "These must be wickedly uncomfortable." He unbuckled the narrow strap.

"Not for the first couple of hours."

He winced. She'd been wearing them since before two this afternoon. No wonder she'd wanted to sit and drink champagne with Mary Lou. He took off the other shoe, and she sighed with relief.

"I shouldn't have asked you to keep them on." He took one of her feet in his hands again and began a slow massage.

"Yes, you should. That's the main reason this kind of shoe exists—to create a sexual fantasy for men. Women often wear them for that exclusive purpose." She moaned softly. "That's nice, Trey."

"I owe it to you." He deepened the massage.

"Hey, I'm the one who chose to wear them. You didn't force me to put them on today." She sighed again. "You're good at this. I shouldn't be surprised."

"Why?" He moved to her other foot.

"Because I already know you have talented hands. You can make that guitar sing. You can make me sing."

"Nice to know." Although that affected him, he wasn't going to indulge the demands of his cock right now. He continued to work on her feet. "Did you bring lotion?"

"There's some in my duffel bag."

Her bag was conveniently on the floor only a couple of feet away. Pulling it over, he handed it up to her. "Would you get it out for me?"

"I know what you're up to, Trey."

"Are you sure?"

"I'm sure." She handed him a tube of lotion. "You're making love to my feet, and then you'll work your way up my legs, and so on."

"So you think massaging your feet is a means to an end?" He squeezed out some sweet-smelling lotion and smoothed it over the arch of her foot.

She shivered. "I do."

"Well, you're right, it is." But he wasn't doing it to prepare her for his future satisfaction. He was doing it because she needed this more than she needed an orgasm. "Just lie back and enjoy it."

"Okay, I will." She settled backward on the bed.

"I like your gold toenail polish."

"The spa here does a nice job." She moaned again. "You could work there. You know your way around a foot massage, cowboy."

"You inspire me." He worked the lotion between her toes. Then he moved to her other foot and gave it the same treatment. He took his time, and the room grew very quiet. Too quiet.

Slowly releasing her foot, he rose to his knees and peered at her. Her eyes were closed, and her breathing was steady. She was asleep.

He chose to be complimented rather than insulted. He'd relaxed her with his foot massage, and she'd felt comfortable enough to drift off. She might be asleep, but they could still share a bed. That would be nice, too. They might not use the condoms he'd left in the nightstand drawer, but he'd be right there beside her all night.

Although he undressed as quietly as he could, he

probably didn't need to worry about waking her up. She slept on. But she couldn't stay like that with her legs hanging off the bed.

Surveying the situation, he mapped out a strategy. He drew back the covers on the far side of the bed. When he leaned over and scooped her up in his arms, she mumbled something and cuddled closer. It sounded like she said, "Has Santa been here?"

He might have misunderstood, but he decided to give her an answer anyway. "Not yet," he murmured as he carried her to the other side of the bed and laid her on the sheet.

Her bathrobe tie had loosened during the transport, and he didn't think she'd want to sleep in that bulky thing, anyway. Working carefully, he slipped each arm out of the sleeves. Getting the thick robe out from under her was a trick, but he finally succeeded.

Grabbing one stolen moment, he gazed at her. She was so much more than a beautiful woman. She had fire and intelligence to spare. If she'd only let him into her life, she'd be so easy to love.

She rolled to her side to face the wall, and he pulled the covers up over her bare shoulder. "Sleep well, sweetheart," he said softly.

"I want skis." The words were distinct this time, even though her eyes remained closed.

He didn't have to think very hard to figure it out. She'd been surrounded by Christmas decorations for days. Then he'd picked her up like a sleeping child and tucked her into bed. In her dream state, she'd asked Santa for a pair of skis. That memory had to have come from somewhere.

Yet she'd told him before that Christmas wasn't par-

ticularly important to her. It had been once, though.
He'd lay money on it. But now she'd rejected every-
thing that was even slightly sentimental, including
Christmas.

Or maybe not. He had a sudden inspiration. If he
could get her to spend Christmas Eve and Christmas
Day at the ranch, he might revive her love of the holiday. He couldn't help thinking that once she surrendered to the joy of the season, she'd be open to loving
him.

That wouldn't solve the problem of her heading
down to Argentina for the summer months, but it
would be a start. She craved the excitement of that
sport, she'd said. All he had to do was present an
option that was at least that exciting. Personally, he
thought loving each other for the rest of their lives fit
the criteria. But that was just him.

Turning out the lights, he climbed into bed beside
her. He wished that he had a Christmas tree like hers
to cast a warm glow as she slept. Her affection for
that tree was another clue that she wasn't quite as im-
mune to the holidays as she let on. But short of getting dressed again and stealing hers, he was out of
luck on that score.

He gathered her close, because he couldn't help
himself. Lying spooned against her, his cock close to
her silky bottom, created a predictable result. He tried
thinking of subjects that would tame his bad boy, but
nothing worked, not even imagining himself naked
in a snowdrift.

A snowdrift had started all this in the first place.
Now he was in bed with his angel, someone who'd
been only a fantasy three days ago. He'd had hot, cre-

ative sex with her. Yet in some ways, even though she was lying right next to him, she seemed out of reach.

His cock twitched because that's what cocks did when they were denied what they wanted. He wasn't going to wake her up so he could get relief, so he rolled to his back with a sigh of frustration. This could be a really long night.

"I'm awake." She rolled to her side, facing him.

Excitement warred with guilt. "My fault. Sorry."

She laid a hand on his chest. "This wasn't supposed to be a slumber party." She stroked him with those tantalizing hands, those provocative, arousing hands.

"I know, but you're tired. You need—"

"You." Reaching down, she circled his stiff cock with sure fingers. Sweet torment. "And you need me," she said. "We decided on this big bed for a reason, and it wasn't so we could sleep better in it."

He turned his head to look at her. "You're mighty persuasive, lady." And he was a sucker for the times when that husky note crept into her voice.

"One more climax apiece," she said. "Then we'll sleep."

When he hesitated, she scooted closer, put her mouth next to his ear and told him what she wanted in two succinct words. He was a goner.

But he refused to take her with the reckless abandon he'd allowed himself before. "Turn me loose, and I'll do exactly what you said." He gently removed her hand from his cock. He wouldn't do exactly what she'd said, though. He had much more in mind than the raw coupling those two words implied.

"Lie back." He reached across her. "Are you okay with the light?"

"Yes." She lifted her head and kissed him full on the mouth, her lips warm and pliant. He got so lost in that kiss that he nearly forgot what he'd been about to do. Her openmouthed, eager kiss shot messages down to his groin. Ah, yes. First the light. Then a condom from the drawer.

He fumbled for the light switch and found it. He'd be damned if he'd love her in the dark and miss watching her expression. Then he grabbed a condom and held on to it while he continued to explore her luscious mouth.

How he loved doing that. She might act skittish when they talked about commitment, but she put her whole heart into her kiss. He tended to believe her kiss more than he believed her words.

He wanted to be inside her, though, and the condom wasn't going to magically attach itself to his cock. Ending the kiss with reluctance, he pulled away long enough to put the doggone thing on. Someday, when his world was arranged the way he'd prefer, he wouldn't have to use them. But that was getting way ahead of the game.

As he moved over her, she looked up at him and seemed about to say something.

"What?"

She shook her head and closed her eyes. "Nothing."

"Please don't close your eyes."

Her lashes fluttered and she looked at him again. "What if I need protection?"

He remembered telling her why he usually wore his hat during a performance. "You don't need to protect yourself from me."

"Are you sure?"

"Absolutely sure." He entered her slowly. This time wasn't about speed and agility or multiple orgasms. This was about celebrating the connection he'd felt since that first moment when he'd discovered her standing in the gift shop.

She sucked in a breath. "When you look at me like that, I...I get scared."

"I told you before." He eased back and slid in again, still moving gently. "You don't have to be afraid of me."

"It's not you I'm afraid of." Her gaze held his. "It's what you make me feel."

"Could that be love?" He stroked her with subtle movements of his hips, arousing her by tiny increments, building the emotion he wanted from her.

"I don't...I don't know."

"I do." He rocked gently within her. "It's this, Elle. This connection between two people."

"It's not that simple." Tears welled in her eyes.

"Yes, it is." He kept loving her, wanting her to feel what he felt.

"No."

"Yes. Two people, finding each other, recognizing each other. The rest is details."

"Oh, Trey." She swallowed. "I wish I could believe you."

"I wish you could, too." He shifted his angle and felt her tighten. "Believe this. We're in tune, Elle. Do you know how rare that is?"

She nodded as tears leaked from the corners of her eyes.

"Then stay with me." He sought the rhythm that

would bring them both joy, and she arched against him as he knew she would. "Stay with me, Elle."

She came apart in his arms, and he followed soon after. But when it was over, he knew that one crucial thing was missing from their special moment. She hadn't promised to stay.

TREY HADN'T PRESSED her for an answer, and for that Elle was grateful. If anything, he pretended that he hadn't said those fateful words "stay with me." He kissed her tenderly before leaving the bed, and when he came back, he turned out the light and gathered her close. In minutes, he was asleep.

But she lay wide-awake, staring into the darkness. She couldn't lead him on anymore. Although she'd warned him from the first that she wasn't interested in anything long-term, he hadn't really accepted that. Instead, he kept trying to find reasons for her to stay in Jackson Hole instead of leaving in April. And tonight he'd made his romantic, loving plea. *Stay with me.*

She wouldn't do that. She wouldn't let herself be carried away by good sex and sweet words and sentimental songs. She wasn't that type.

But he was, and he needed someone who *would* allow herself to be carried away, who'd agree with his romantic belief in soul mates and destiny. Maybe he'd find another musician who could share his fascination with acoustical sex. They could have fun singing duets like the one he'd performed with Tyler.

Elle had toyed with the idea of continuing to see him after this long weekend was over. But when he'd asked her to stay, she'd faced reality. They had different goals.

The longer she indulged herself with this hot affair, the tougher life would be for Trey when she broke it off. He'd mourn losing her the way he'd mourned losing Cassie, which would sideline him for weeks or months. If she cared about him, she should minimize his pain, not prolong it.

But telling him that now, when he was celebrating with his friends, also would be cruel. He'd need some private time to work through the disappointment, and he wouldn't have that opportunity until the group went back to the ranch. She'd have to pretend all was well until he left on Tuesday. That wouldn't be particularly easy, but she'd do it for his sake.

She wondered if stress would keep her awake all night, but she was already sleep-deprived, and finally exhaustion claimed her. When she woke up a few hours later, Trey was in the shower, whistling. That broke her heart.

He was so cute when he was happy, and she wanted him to be happy. That meant exiting his life and leaving space for someone who fit into his world and his dreams. Someone who wasn't her.

Toweling himself off, he came out of the bathroom and grinned at her. "Better move it, sweetheart, if you still plan to teach a bunch of yokels to ski this morning."

She scrambled out of bed and pulled her phone out of her duffel. "Yikes." It was later than she'd thought, but that was better. No time for conversation about delicate topics.

"I thought I'd let you sleep a little longer, so I took first shower. It's all yours. I'm finished in there."

"Thank you." As she passed by him on the way

into the bathroom, he caught her around the waist and pulled her close.

"Good morning to you, too." He gave her a quick kiss and looked into her eyes. "Listen, about what I said last night, I probably shouldn't have—"

"Don't worry about it." She managed a smile. "You got carried away."

"Right." His gaze searched hers, and he gave her a little squeeze. "You'd better hop in the shower."

"Yep!" She heard the note of false cheer in her voice and hoped he hadn't noticed. She hurried into the bathroom. "I forgot to ask if you have ski pants for today," she called over her shoulder.

"Rented them yesterday morning. And a jacket. All the guys will be in better shape this morning. You'll be impressed."

"I'm sure I will." She turned on the shower, which cut off any further discussion. So far, so good.

But it was still early in the day. She had to get through the rest of it, including tonight, without giving Trey a hint that she was planning to end their affair tomorrow. Given how perceptive he was, she might be asking the impossible.

_16_

HE'D BLOWN IT. Trey had been afraid that he'd over-
played his hand by asking her to stay. But the lovemaking had been so sweet, and he'd thought the timing
was right. Obviously it hadn't been and might never
be. He wouldn't ever know, because he'd been impatient, exactly what Watkins had warned him about.

Impatience was a failing of his, with the excep-
tion of his work with horses. He could be patient as
all get-out with horses, because he made allowances
for the language barrier. But communication should
be easier between people.

It wasn't, though, and his lack of patience with that
might have cost him Elle. All through the ski lesson he
berated himself for not taking things slower. He'd had
until *April,* for God's sake. Rome wasn't conquered in
a day, as they said. He shouldn't have tried to capture
Elle's heart in a weekend.

But he'd pushed the issue, and she'd decided her
answer was no. She probably wouldn't tell him until
tomorrow. She'd want to give him a chance to go home
and lick his wounds.

That gave him a choice of pretending right along with her and sharing a bed with her tonight or breaking up with her now. Both options sucked. If he went along with her game, he'd get to hold her for one more night. But the whole time he'd be waiting for the ax to fall.

Debating the issue while trying to control a couple of skinny waxed boards on a very slippery slope meant he fell down a lot. He used up his entire vocabulary of swear words and invented a few more. Jack came gliding by when Trey was berating his *pucking foles*.

Jack executed a perfect hockey stop. "What the hell are pucking foles?"

Trey struggled to his feet, yet again. "It's from the Latin."

"Doesn't sound like Latin to me." Then his frown cleared. "Okay, I get it. Your pucking foles are driving you nucking futs. Am I right?"

Trey stood in the pizza slice position and adjusted his goggles. "You are so right, my friend."

"Listen, it might be my imagination, but you seem a little off this morning."

"I'm fine."

"If you say so. But Elle doesn't seem quite herself, either. I'm thinking there might be a connection."

Trey gazed at Jack. "I know you're my boss and all, but…"

"You wish I'd mind my own business?"

"Something like that. I was trying to find a more diplomatic way of saying it."

"I wouldn't be butting in at all, except that I already sort of did."

Trey's chest tightened. "Like how?"

"Trying to be Santa Claus. Seeing how well you two were getting along, I checked with Carl about Elle's work schedule, and he's fine with her taking Christmas Eve and Christmas morning off. So I invited her to the ranch for the night."

"What—" Trey had to stop and clear his throat. "What did she say?"

"That she couldn't make it. Too many obligations here. I told her I'd spoken with Carl, and then she made some other lame excuse about needing to call her folks that night, and they're over in Germany, and it's complicated, blah, blah, blah."

"I guarantee she made that up. She doesn't want to come to the ranch."

"Why not? I thought you two—"

"Nope."

"Since when?"

Pain sliced through his heart. "Last night. Technically, early this morning." That's when he'd opened his big mouth and killed his chances.

"I'm sorry." Jack sighed. "That sucks." He glanced at Trey. "You sure? Because sometimes a woman acts as if she wants one thing, but she really wants something else."

"I wish that could be the case, but it's not. Anyway, thanks for trying." He desperately wished to change the subject. "Nice outfit, by the way."

"I'm rather fond of it, myself." Jack's ski pants and jacket were solid black except for a red stripe down the side of the pants and along the length of each sleeve. He'd chosen to go with a red-and-black headband instead of a hat, which suited a guy who was part Shoshone. His iridescent goggles must have set him back a tidy sum, but they made him look like an Olympian.

"Are you thinking you'll get into this skiing thing, then?"

"I just might. I'm usually a little bored in the winter. I've considered building an indoor riding arena, which would help, but I couldn't do that until next summer. If I drove up here a couple of times a week and practiced with Elle, I might get the hang of it."

"You might." Trey cursed himself all over again. He could have done the same exact thing and taken his time wooing Elle.

"You could ride up with me."

"That won't work. Not now."

"Hellfire, cowboy. You must have really put your foot in it."

"Yeah, I did." Trey glanced over at Elle, who'd acquired a new pupil this morning. Redheaded Cassidy O'Connelli, wobbly on a pair of skis, moved slowly down the slope with Elle skiing just as slowly right beside her. It hurt to watch Elle, who was at her best teaching a beginner to ski, so he looked away. "And I don't think there's a damned thing I can do about it now."

ELLE HOPED THAT Trey's inability to concentrate on the skiing lesson was from lack of sleep. She didn't think it was. He knew something had changed with her, and he was no dummy. He could figure out why.

She also hoped Trey hadn't been behind Jack's invitation to the ranch. Asking if Trey had requested that invitation would have opened up a can of worms, so she hadn't. In any case, Jack was certain to relay her response, which would give Trey further proof that the relationship was about to end.

If he'd put Jack up to asking, then she was definitely doing the right thing by backing away. She wasn't going to be pressured by Trey or the Chance family. She'd built a life that suited her, and abandoning it on a whim wasn't her style.

The lesson ran long because nobody was ready to quit, so it was late morning before everyone started packing up. Cassidy still wanted more instruction, but Elle thought the girl needed a break between sessions. As they worked out a time to meet that afternoon, Trey approached, his skis balanced on one broad shoulder. She'd bet he could hardly wait to get rid of them. If today was any indication, skiing wasn't his thing.

He waited until Cassidy left, but once she did, he wasted no time on pleasantries. "Do you have some free time this afternoon?"

Judging from his expression, he wasn't asking because he wanted to race to his room and have sex. "I have a little time. Cassidy wants to come back out around three."

"After lunch, then?"

"Not right after. There's the send-off for Pam and Emmett. I'm sure you want to be there for that."

"Yeah, I do. I'd forgotten about it."

That he'd forgotten the send-off was another sign that he was very distracted. She had a bad feeling about why he wanted to see her this afternoon.

"So after Pam and Emmett leave, are you free?"

"I should be. Alex and Jeb want another lesson, and we settled on four, if the weather holds. But I'm not booked between the send-off and Cassie's lesson

at three." She sounded like a CEO juggling appoint-
ments, but that couldn't be helped. Now that the stay
was almost over, a few people wanted to cram in more
time on skis, and she was thrilled about that.

He gave her a wry smile. "Glad you can fit me in."

"Could this wait until after I'm finished with Jeb
and Alex?"

He hesitated. "Not really. I thought we might take
a walk, if that's okay with you."

"Sure. That sounds nice." Whatever this discussion
would be about, she could tell he wanted it over with.
A knot formed in her stomach.

"Great. If you're going to the send-off, we can meet
up there."

"I thought I'd go. They won't care if I'm there, probably, but...yes, I'd like to see them off."

"I'll meet you afterward, then." He started to leave.

"Trey?"

"Yeah?" He turned back to her, and there was a
tiny spark in his eyes, as if some unnamed hope had
been momentarily ignited.

"Did you ask Jack to invite me to the ranch for
Christmas?" She couldn't help asking. Before they
took that walk, she needed to know.

The spark died. "Nope. That was all his idea."

Although she was relieved to hear it, she hated seeing the light leave his dark gaze. "I appreciate being
asked, but I can't make it. It's complicated, but I—"

"I understand, Elle. See you after Pam and Emmett leave."

When he was gone, she stared at the snowy hillside
for a long time. She felt like such a louse. If only she'd
followed her instincts in the first place and steered

clear of this man, they'd both have been spared a lot of pain.

A few minutes later, as she was headed back to the lodge, Jared called out to her.

She turned around. "Did I forget to put something away?" In her current frame of mind, that was possible.

"Nope. Everything's shipshape. Did you eat breakfast?"

"Never got around to it."

"Me, either. Want to go see if there's anything left in the kitchen?"

"Sure." She might as well. Although she wasn't particularly hungry, she ought to eat. It could be a long day.

Jared fell into step beside her. "So, everything okay with you?"

"Yes." She glanced at him. "Why?"

"Just wondered. A while ago you were staring off into space as if there'd been a death in the family. And Trey didn't smile much this morning."

"I'm sure he wasn't smiling. He wiped out a lot today."

"I noticed. But you two are okay, right?"

"We have some issues, but it'll be fine."

"I'm glad to hear it, because he's really good for you."

Elle blinked. Jared wasn't in the habit of making personal comments. "What's that supposed to mean?"

"Don't take this wrong, but you keep people at a distance. You're different with him, though. It's nice to see."

She stared at him. "I do not keep people at a distance."

"Yeah, you do, Elle. You're sweet and friendly and a good teacher. But it's like there's an invisible force field around you. Except this weekend, not so much. I figure that's because of him."

Her chest tightened. If that was true, then she'd made a big mess for herself as well as for Trey. But she didn't want Jared to know how his comments had rocked her back. "You're scaring me. Since when did you turn into Dr. Phil?"

That made him laugh. "I know, right? Totally out of character. Blame it on the fact that I watched *The Muppet Christmas Carol* last night on TV. Now I'm all introspective about the meaning of life."

"You're not comparing me to Scrooge, are you?"

"*No.* Nothing like that. Forget I said anything. Sheesh. This is why I don't get into the touchy-feely stuff."

"We'll pretend it never happened." As if she could. Now she'd be obsessing over what he'd said, damn it.

"Good. By the way, they want us to make another teaching video whenever we can work it in. I'm thinking this week would be good. Maybe Wednesday afternoon. The schedule's kind of loose on Wednesday."

"Wednesday would be great." She welcomed a change of subject, and filling her calendar with activities was a good idea. If Jared was right, and she'd let down her guard and fallen for Trey, even a little bit, then she had some recalibrating to do. Keeping busy would be her salvation.

TREY STOOD WITH Watkins and Mary Lou in the crowd of well-wishers gathered in the front driveway of the resort. A long black limo sat under the portico and a uniformed driver stood by the passenger door, waiting. Everyone had been given a bottle of bubbles as a send-off gesture.

The bride and groom had not yet arrived, so Trey had time to scan the crowd for Elle. She wasn't here. She'd said she was coming, though. And after the limo drove away... He swallowed hard when he thought of the discussion ahead of him.

Mary Lou put a hand on the sleeve of his sheepskin jacket. "Where's Elle?"

"Don't know."

"She's coming, isn't she?"

"She said she would."

"Trey, look at me."

That almost made him smile. Mary Lou had adopted a parental tone with him, and he loved it. He glanced down at her. "Yes, ma'am?"

"Did you two have a fight?"

"No."

"Well, *something's* wrong. I can tell by the—oh, wait. Here she comes."

Trey had spotted her, too. She hurried out of the resort entrance door, pulling on her ski jacket as she came. He would love to say that his heart didn't ache like hell at the sight of her. He couldn't say that.

She smiled as she walked over to where he stood with Watkins and Mary Lou. "I'm glad I didn't miss them. Time got away from me."

"You don't have any bubbles," Mary Lou said. "They handed them out earlier."

"Take mine." Trey held out his bottle.

"That's okay. I'll—"

"Take it, Elle."

She met his gaze. Something in his voice or in his eyes must have communicated his frustration with this entire situation. She must have decided he was nearing the end of his rope, because she took the bottle. "Thanks. That's generous of you."

A cheer went up, and Trey broke eye contact with Elle. "Here they come." Then he gasped. "Good Lord, she's got him in a white linen suit and a Panama hat. I can't believe it."

Mary Lou laughed with delight. "I love it! Look at Pam, all in pastels. They're ready for the tropics. That's just the cutest thing ever."

"I don't know," Watkins said. "Emmett's never worn anything but jeans and cowboy shirts. He's not gonna recognize himself in the mirror."

"Give him a week," Mary Lou said. "Don't forget that you were wearing shorts and gaudy shirts by the second day of our cruise."

"Yeah, but Emmett's not even there yet and he already looks like he owns a sugar plantation."

"I think it's great," Trey said. "Good for Emmett. Two days ago he was ready to ditch the ceremony and head for Vegas. Now look at him."

"He's doing it for love," Mary Lou said.

"And for nooky," Watkins added.

"Watkins." Mary Lou punched his arm, but she laughed all the same.

"Nothing wrong with having a double motivation." Trey glanced sideways at Elle. Hard to tell what she was thinking, but she didn't seem to be enjoying the conversation the way the rest of them were.

Emmett and Pam stood on the top step giving hugs

and handshakes to family members clustered around them. Then they turned toward the limo.

"Get your bubbles ready," Mary Lou said. "It's time."

The driver opened the door. Hand-in-hand, Emmett and Pam hurried down the steps in a shower of iridescent bubbles. Once they were tucked inside the limo, everyone followed the car a little ways down the drive, waving and blowing more bubbles.

Throughout the send-off, Trey kept track of Elle. She'd blown bubbles along with everyone else, but her shouts of good cheer had sounded hollow to him. That might be his mood, though.

After the limo pulled away from the resort, he glanced down at her. "Ready for that walk?"

"Sure." She started to tuck the bottle in her jacket pocket. "Oh, do you want these back?" She took the bottle out again.

"You can keep it."

"All right. Some of the younger skiers might have fun creating bubbles going downhill. Where are we walking?"

"I'd hoped you'd make a suggestion. You know the area better than I do." Their careful formality sliced him to ribbons.

"This way, then." She started across the driveway.

He walked beside her in silence. He'd rather not say his piece where they might have an audience. Within about five minutes they'd entered a groomed trail that wound through the trees.

"This is for cross-country skiing," Elle said. "We have a few guests who've asked for that over the years, so Carl built a small trail for them. Nobody will be on it now."

"I wonder if cross-country would suit me better." His boots crunched on the packed snow, but he didn't sink in.

"It might, at that."

"I don't suppose you care much for it, though. Too tame."

"It's okay for a change of pace." Her steps kept time with his.

"Maybe I'll check it out." He didn't know why he was discussing this. Procrastination, probably. They were out of sight of the resort. The air was still and cold. Then a breeze sighed through the pines, and ahead of them, a branch showered snow onto the path.

He stopped and turned to her. "Elle, I pushed you with that request last night, and I realize it set you off. You've decided there's no hope for us, and if that's the case, I'm ready to cut my losses." He watched her eyes, hoping against hope that he'd see denial there.

Instead, she gazed at him with sad resignation. "It's for the best, Trey. I'm not the one for you. I pray that you find her someday, and that she's as romantic and loving as you are. You deserve that."

So that was it, then. He wished an avalanche would come along and bury him under it. But he wouldn't want her to be buried under it, too, so he couldn't really wish that.

Instead, he had to man up and get through this. Except he wasn't sure what to do next. Shake hands? Give her a farewell kiss? No, that was out. One kiss and he was liable to do something stupid, like beg her to change her mind.

She looked away and cleared her throat. "Maybe we should walk back."

"Uh, yeah. You go ahead. You have that lesson with Cassidy. I'll stay out a little longer."

She glanced up, her blue eyes moist. "You're sure?"

"Elle, I won't get lost."

"Okay, then. Goodbye, Trey." She looked as if she might touch him, but then she didn't. "Goodbye." She walked away from him, her pace faster this time, her feet making a noise like a popcorn machine.

He stared after her, his whole body aching. Then he turned and walked in the other direction, because that was easier than standing still. He'd promised her he wouldn't get lost. But he'd never felt so lost in his life.

17

ELLE MANAGED TO avoid Trey for the rest of the time the Last Chance folks were at the resort. Doing that kept her on edge. She didn't sleep well, either, knowing he was there. She woke up in the middle of the night, certain he'd knocked on her door, but no one was outside when she looked.

She told herself that once Trey had left, she'd be able to relax. Instead, she got the flu, or what felt like the flu. She didn't run a fever or get sick to her stomach, but she ached all over. A soak in the hot tub didn't help. A massage didn't help. Getting drunk with Amy didn't help.

As the two of them sat in Amy's room working on their second bottle of wine, Amy listened to Elle describe her peculiar symptoms. "Is there a chance you're in love with the guy?" she asked. "Could that be what ails you?"

Elle's head jerked up. "Hell, no!"

"Don't look so horrified. That would explain why you feel so rotten. You're in love with him. It's possible."

"No, it's not possible. Not after four days."

"So you don't believe he's in love with you, either?"

She shook her head violently. Too violently. She had to put her hand over her eyes and take a deep breath. "Whoa. Dizzy."

"Not to mention that you overreacted to the question. I think maybe—"

"Nope, nope." Elle held up her hand like a traffic cop. "Trey is not in love with me. He's in love with the angel who came to his rescue. He's a romantic dreamer who fell in love with an idea, not a flesh-and-blood woman."

"Hmm."

"What?"

"I watched him at the reception. I watched both of you. If he wasn't a man in love, he gave a damned good impression of it. You seemed to be into him, too."

"Amy, you were seeing what you wanted to see."

"That is so not the case. First of all, I wish he hadn't been so stuck on you, because I would have dated him in a heartbeat. Second, I was fascinated by the change in you. You can deny it all you want, but you acted way happier when he was around. More open, somehow."

Elle frowned. That sounded too much like Jared's comment. "So I've been closed in the past?"

"That sounds bad. I didn't mean that in a critical way."

"Jared said I don't let people get close to me."

Amy's gaze was filled with compassion. "That's sort of true. Part of it is that you're only here for six months. I just start getting to know you again, and you're gone. But...I have the feeling that's on purpose.

By going somewhere else for six months, you don't get too attached to the place or the people."

Elle didn't know what to say about that, especially because Amy might have scored a bull's-eye. "It's... it's what I'm used to."

"I know, hon. When you grow up like that, always on the move, it becomes a habit. But if you've fallen for this guy, and I think you have, then maybe it's time to break that habit."

"That scares me to death."

"I'll bet."

Elle held out her glass. "More wine, please. I'm not ready to examine this concept sober. Not yet, anyway."

Amy poured wine for both of them. Then she picked up her glass. "Here's to facing down fears."

"Maybe." Elle raised her glass. "To quote Scarlett, I'll think about that tomorrow."

But she didn't. The next day she rejected the idea that she was jetting between continents because she was afraid to let herself become attached to people and places. What nonsense. Unfortunately, her mysterious aches and pains refused to go away. She took aspirin and pretended she was fine.

Three days before Christmas, Dominique Chance emailed a link to the wedding pictures along with a chatty note about the fun they'd had at Serenity. Elle put off opening the link for another day. She wanted to see the pictures, but also knew Trey would be in them.

When she woke up at four in the morning on Christmas Eve Day with a burning desire to look at those pictures, she surrendered to the urge to click on that link. For the next hour, she sat on her bed and watched a slide show of the wedding.

Some shots made her laugh, but others…well, she had to hit Pause, climb out of bed and grab the tissue box. It wasn't only the pictures of Trey that made her cry, either. She teared up at the tender scene of Jack holding Archie at the altar, and the loving expression on Emmett's face as Pam walked toward him down the aisle.

She got weepy when she came to the image of Pam and Emmett dancing at the reception. And then…there she was in Trey's arms when they'd waltzed to "If I Didn't Have You in My Life." Dominique had several shots from different angles, as if she hadn't wanted Elle to miss the message.

She didn't miss it. Trey gazed down at her in the same way Emmett had looked at Pam. But that wasn't all. Dominique had captured the emotion on Elle's face with stunning clarity, too.

It was a portrait of a woman in love. Jetting from continent to continent hadn't worked this time. She'd become attached to Trey Wheeler, and if she ever wanted this horrible ache to stop, she had to admit that attachment and honor it. Her roving days were over.

TREY VOWED THAT he was going to enjoy his first Christmas at the Last Chance and put all thoughts of Elle clean out of his mind. Around four in the afternoon he left the bunkhouse. The other hands were taking their sweet time getting showered and dressed for the big night, but Trey was eager to join the party.

A light snow fell as he took the short walk uphill to the massive two-story log structure that was the heart and soul of the ranch. According to Watkins and Mary Lou, the house had begun as a two-story box shape.

As the family had grown, a wing had been added on each side, canted outward so the house seemed to be reaching out its arms in welcome.

A covered porch ran along the entire length. In summer, the porch was lined with rockers and became a good spot for socializing. But winter was not the time for rocking on the porch. Winter meant gathering around the giant stone fireplace in the living room, and that's what Trey looked forward to.

Most folks had arrived, judging by all the vehicles parked near the house. Although the Chance brothers each had a house of their own on ranch property, they'd all driven the few miles to the main house and would spend the night here, along with their wives and kids.

They'd be the only ones to stay overnight, but there'd be plenty of other guests. Josie's brother, Alex Keller, and his wife, Tyler, would be here. Trey wanted to ask her about recording a few songs, just to see what would happen if they put them out there. He planned to train horses for the rest of his life, but a little extra income never hurt.

Nash Bledsoe's truck was parked with the others, so he and his wife, Bethany, had driven over from the Triple G, a small ranch that bordered the Last Chance. Bethany wrote motivational books. Trey didn't know her well yet, and he'd had no opportunity to talk with her at the wedding, either. But gatherings like this one were a good place to get acquainted.

No doubt other members of the Chances' extended family would show up, too. Jack's half brothers, Wyatt and Rafe Locke, along with their wives, had promised to make it. Neither couple had been able to attend the wedding, so they were adamant they'd be at the Christmas Eve party.

Trey figured he was forgetting several other folks who would be there, too. Good thing the house was big and Mary Lou had cooked a whole bunch of food. Watkins said she'd been cheerfully slaving away in the kitchen for two days. Apparently, she liked nothing better than preparing for a party.

Lights glowed from every window, and as Trey approached, snatches of Christmas music filtered outside. A huge wreath hung on the front door, and two miniature trees with sparkling lights stood on either side of it. When the temperature dipped lower tonight, those little trees would be brought in so the lights wouldn't pop in the cold, but Sarah loved making the entrance festive.

Trey had told himself not to think about Elle, but damn, he wished she could see this. She might not fall in love with him, but she'd have to fall in love with this big old ranch house and the wonderful people inside, celebrating the season. She wasn't here, though, and that was her loss.

Taking a deep breath of crisp air, he walked up the steps and opened the door. Inside, the scene was even better than Trey had imagined. The noise level was high, with a mixture of Christmas music, conversation and laughter—it was a happy noise. A few people sat on the comfortable leather furniture, but most of them stood so they could move around and talk to everyone.

A graceful wooden staircase spiraled to the second floor. Trey noticed little Archie navigating his way down the stairs, a Barbie doll clutched in his pudgy fist. About the time he reached the bottom step, Sarah Bianca raced down the upstairs hallway. "Archie! No!"

Archie looked at Trey, pure mischief in his expression, before taking off toward the crowded living room.

"Archie!" Sarah Bianca pounded down the stairs in hot pursuit.

As Trey watched the drama unfold, Jack snatched up his son and took him over to admire the lights on the giant tree in the corner. While Archie was distracted by the lights, Jack quietly took the doll away. Gabe put a hand on Sarah Bianca's tiny shoulder, steered her toward Jack, and retrieved the doll. His daughter marched back upstairs, and all was well.

Trey had often wondered if Jack and Gabe's work with horses carried over to their method of child care. If so, he might turn out to be a pretty good dad himself. But that thought reminded him of Elle and their failed love affair.

"Hey, cowboy, no long faces tonight." Watkins approached him, a beer in each hand. He gave one to Trey. "Merry Christmas, son."

Even though Watkins's use of *son* put a lump in Trey's throat, he wouldn't ever want the older man to quit saying it. He smiled. "Same to you, Watkins. Cheers. How's Mary Lou doing in the kitchen?"

"Just fine, but I'm fixing to go back and help her and Cassidy. I wanted to make sure you had a beer, though, before I left the area."

"I'll come and help, too."

"Nah, you don't have to do that. Stay out here. Have fun. Get you some munchies."

"I can do that in a little while. Let's go." He started

down the hallway that led to the dining room and kitchen area.

"Okay, if you insist." Watkins walked along beside him. "This is a big crowd, bigger than usual, so Sarah's asked Mary Lou to set up a buffet in the dining room instead of trying to serve the food in the living room, like they used to do."

"Makes sense. I— Whoops, there's my phone. I don't know why I brought it. Habit, I guess. If we hadn't walked down here I doubt I would have heard it." He couldn't imagine who'd be calling him. Maybe some cowboy from his old job, wanting to wish him a happy holiday.

Then he stared at the readout in disbelief. "Oh, my God."

Watkins's swift glance was filled with concern. "What's wrong?"

"I don't know. Elle's calling. Excuse me a minute." Heart pounding, he put the phone to his ear. "Elle?"

"Trey, I can't believe this. I'm stuck in a snowdrift."

His heart beat faster. "Are you okay?"

"I'm fine, but this truck isn't going anywhere without a tow."

For the life of him, he couldn't figure out why she was calling him. "Where are you?"

"On the road to the Last Chance."

"What?" Then he said the first stupid thing that popped into his head. "What the hell are you doing there?"

"I was coming to see you, and I don't know the road, and it's dark out here, and it's snowing, and I somehow lost track of where the road was."

"You were coming to see *me? Why?"

"Because I—listen, instead of telling you all this on the phone, could you come and pull me out? Then I can follow you to the ranch."

"Yeah, sure. I'll be right there. See you soon." He disconnected the phone and looked at Watkins. "She's stuck out on the ranch road."

"So I gathered." Watkins clapped him on the back. "Looks promising, son."

"Maybe." Trey was afraid to hope for too much. "I need to go pull her out. I know I offered to help you and Mary Lou, but—"

"Don't give it another thought. But can I offer a suggestion?"

"Like what?"

"Don't take your Jeep out there. You'll be fumbling around in the dark, and when you're done, you'll still be in one vehicle and she'll be in another, which isn't very romantic. Save the towing for when it's daylight."

"And do what?"

"Rescue her the cowboy way. Ride out there on a horse and bring her back tucked in front of you. You have the advantage, son. Maximize it."

ELLE PONDERED THE irony of her situation as she watched for headlights on the road. Maybe it wasn't ironic, after all, but fitting. Supposedly she'd saved Trey's life last spring, but by doing so, she'd apparently saved her own.

Without realizing it, she'd blindly followed a pattern stamped into her by her parents. They'd adjusted to constant moves by becoming detached from people and places. Or maybe they'd chosen their life paths because they preferred to stay detached.

She wasn't like them. Trey had shown her that by jolting her out of a numbing lifestyle and making her feel again. She'd needed a dyed-in-the-wool romantic to accomplish that, and she'd found him.

But getting to him tonight had been more of a challenge than she'd anticipated. Honest to God, they needed streetlights on this road. She'd never driven in such total blackness. If Trey hadn't answered his cell phone, her predicament could have been dire.

He had, though, and he should arrive any minute. She'd left her headlights on so he'd see her. Beyond the reach of those beams, she searched for evidence that he was coming in her direction.

Then her phone rang. Why the hell was he calling her? She pushed the connect button. "Where are you? I have my lights on. I shouldn't be hard to spot."

"I decided to warn you that I'm not coming in my truck."

"What do you mean, you're not coming?" She sounded panicky, but she couldn't help it. Darkness surrounded her, not to mention snow, and she needed to be rescued, damn it!

"I'm heading toward you, but I'm riding a horse. I didn't want to scare you."

"A *horse?*" She wondered if this was a crazy dream. "What is it, a Clydesdale?"

"No, just a regular horse named Inkspot. We're going to leave your truck here until tomorrow when it'll be easier to see what we're doing. Inkspot and I will take you to the ranch."

"You're kidding, right?"

"Nope." And he rode into the beam of her headlights.

She stared at this broad-shouldered cowboy wearing a sheepskin jacket and a Stetson. He'd come to her rescue, not like the Lone Ranger, but like a knight in shining armor, mounted on a magnificent black-and-white horse.

Grabbing her duffel, she opened the door and climbed out as he dismounted. They met in the beam of her headlights, and she launched herself into his arms, knocking his hat into the snow.

He didn't seem to notice as he gathered her close and kissed her. His mouth was cold at first, but it warmed up fast. And all the while, she was thinking that this was the man she would be kissing for the rest of her life, and that was beyond wonderful.

Although he couldn't seem to stop kissing her, he managed to lift his mouth long enough to murmur a few words about needing to get her back to the ranch. Maybe that was so, but she had what she wanted right here.

Finally, he cupped her face and put some distance between her lips and his. "Seriously. We have to get back. It's cold out here."

"I hadn't noticed."

"Trust me, you will. Let's turn off your headlights and lock your Jeep."

"Not before I say what I came to say." Suddenly it seemed more important than anything else.

He went very still. "Okay."

"I love you, Trey Wheeler. I've never been in love before, so I didn't know what had happened to me, but you happened to me, and I've been an idiot, and—" She didn't get to finish because he started kissing her again. But she'd said most of it, at least.

Moments later, he came up for air. "That's the most beautiful speech I've ever heard."

"There's more."

"And I can't wait to hear it. But if we don't get back soon, they'll send out a search party, and that will louse up everyone's Christmas Eve celebration."

"I don't want that."

"Me, either."

"But I just need to hear one thing from you before we go."

"Anything. I'll say anything you want me to."

"Come on, Trey. You know what it is. You write songs about it."

"Are you talking about saying that I love you? Isn't it obvious?"

"Yes." She laughed. "But that doesn't mean a girl doesn't want to hear those words when she's driven all the way out here in the dark on Christmas Eve."

He cupped the back of her neck with one gloved hand and gazed into her eyes. "I love you, Elle Masterson. I love you with everything I have, everything I am and everything I will ever be."

"Oh." Tears filled her eyes. "That's…beautiful."

"Not nearly as beautiful as the life we're going to have together." He brushed his warm lips over hers. "Starting right now." In moments he'd locked her Jeep and hoisted her into the saddle in true hero fashion.

And although they rode off into the snow instead of into the sunset, Elle had no doubt they would have a very happy ending.

Epilogue

"Guess we won't have to spend Christmas Eve delivering a foal, after all." Regan O'Connelli stripped off his rubber gloves and got to his feet.

Timothy Lindquist, head trainer for the Marley Stables, sighed. "Sorry to bring you out here for a false alarm, Doc. I thought for sure she was in labor. The boss has high hopes for this one, up to and including the Triple Crown, so I can't take chances."

"I completely understand. But my fiancée will be very happy not to spend Christmas Eve alone."

Timothy grinned. "Same with my wife. She knows how important this foal is, but she still grumbled when I informed her that this was the night."

"Not from what I see, but I'd keep an eye on things if I were you." Regan picked up his bag.

"Don't worry. I will. But coming down here every few hours is a hell of a lot better than spending the night in the barn. Thanks, Doc."

"You bet." Regan shook the trainer's hand. "Call me if you notice any changes."

"Got your number in my phone. Merry Christmas."

"Same to you." Regan left the barn and glanced up at the clear sky. No snow in sight. Too bad.

In Virginia, you never knew if you'd have snow for the holidays or not. Jeannette was hoping for a white Christmas, and it didn't look promising. But she'd probably trade snow for having him around tonight. He'd told her he'd probably be gone for hours, maybe all night.

On the drive home he pulled out his phone to call and let her know he was on his way. He was in the habit of doing that. Then he thought better of it. Since it was Christmas, he'd surprise her. That would be more romantic.

But now that he had his phone out, he could call his sister Cassidy in Wyoming and wish her a Merry Christmas. So far she seemed to love apprenticing as the housekeeper at the Last Chance, plus she got to see Tyler and Morgan a lot, and Cassidy adored her big sisters.

With seven siblings, plus his parents, Regan had to space out his holiday calls. He'd contact both Tyler and Morgan tomorrow, when he had more time. He wanted all the details on the wedding, especially Tyler's performances with Watkins and Trey Wheeler.

Talking to Morgan would take a while, too, because it would undoubtedly include a long conversation with his niece Sarah Bianca. He smiled. He was crazy about that little redhead.

Cassidy answered right away. "Regan! Merry Christmas! I can't talk long, because we have this *huge* party going on. I'll text you about it later."

"Great! So you're having fun?"

"Are you kidding? I *love* it here. Love, love, love

it. You should move out to Jackson Hole, Regan. Nick keeps saying he needs a partner in his vet business."

Regan laughed. "Yeah, he mentioned that when I was there last summer, but Cass, I have a partner, remember? Drake wouldn't appreciate having me bail on him, and I wouldn't, anyway. He's my best friend."

"I know." Cassidy sighed dramatically. "But it would be so cool if you were here, too. You and Drake could both come!"

"'Fraid not. His folks live here, and they helped us build our practice. Then there's Jeannette. Her family's here, too. I guarantee she wouldn't want to move to Wyoming."

"Well, bummer. Promise you'll come out for a visit soon, okay? Bring Jeannette. Maybe once she sees the place, she'll be hooked."

"I'll see what I can figure out, sweetie." But he didn't know when he'd work in a visit to the Last Chance. He and Jeannette were deep into wedding planning. He'd suggested Jackson Hole for their honeymoon, and she'd made a face.

"Gotta go, brother of mine. Mary Lou needs me. Merry Christmas!"

"Merry Christmas, Cassidy. Love you." As he disconnected, his chest tightened with longing. He could imagine how festive the ranch house was tonight.

But he couldn't be in two places at once, and he had a hot woman waiting in the town house they'd rented temporarily until they decided for sure where they wanted to buy. He was almost there. She'd be so excited to see him.

As he turned down the street, he noticed Drake's SUV parked in front of the house. Huh. Then he chuckled. Drake had dropped by with his last-minute gift. Typical of the guy. Drake bragged about his Christmas Eve shopping marathons. Jeannette had probably offered him a beer.

Regan parked in the street instead of pulling into the drive. This would be fun. He'd surprise them both, and then the three of them could have a Christmas Eve drink together. Perfect.

Pleased with how the evening was turning out, he strode up the walk, climbed the steps and unlocked the front door. When he walked in, he expected to see both of them sitting in the living room, but it was empty. Maybe they'd gone back to the kitchen, although it was really quiet back there.

Then he heard a sound he knew quite well, one that he'd become fond of in the past six months. The wail drifting down from their upstairs bedroom was unmistakable. Someone had just given his fiancée an orgasm. And the odds were excellent that it was the same person who drove the SUV parked outside.

* * * * *

COMING NEXT MONTH FROM

HARLEQUIN® *Blaze*®

Available December 17, 2013

#779 UNFORGETTABLE
Unrated!
Samantha Hunter

After an explosion leaves firefighter Erin Riley with nearly complete amnesia, she has no recollection of her former lover, Bo Myers, the fire investigator on her case. But their strong attraction is something she can't deny....

#780 TEXAS OUTLAWS: JESSE
The Texas Outlaws
Kimberly Raye

Jesse James Chisholm is back in Lost Gun, Texas, and he intends to do whatever it takes to bring out the bad girl in Gracie Stone before she hangs up her wild and wicked ways for good!

#781 STILL SO HOT!
Serena Bell

Dating coach Elisa Henderson is ready for anything when she accompanies her new client to the Caribbean—anything, that is, except her onetime friend and almost lover Brett Jordan. Suddenly it's not just the island temperature heating things up!

#782 MY SECRET FANTASIES
Forbidden Fantasies
Joanne Rock

I was about to realize my two biggest dreams—opening a shop on the coast, and penning a steamy novel. But the sexy owner refused to sell his property to me. And the hero of my book began to resemble him more and more....

REQUEST YOUR FREE BOOKS!
2 FREE NOVELS PLUS 2 FREE GIFTS!

HARLEQUIN

Blaze®

red-hot reads!

HBI3R2

Enjoy this sizzling sneak peek of

Unforgettable

by Samantha Hunter.

Available December 17
wherever Harlequin books are sold.

"Forget it," Erin said flatly, trying to step around him. "I'm never going back to being a firefighter, ever. We both know it."

The night air lifted her scent. It surrounded him, mixing with the sweet evening aromas of fresh grass and recent rain. Though distracted, he reached out, stopping her again. He knew he shouldn't.

"So now what? What next?" he asked.

They were close. She looked up at him, and the irritation in her face disappeared. Bo didn't know if it was his imagination or wishful thinking, but heat arced between them like it had back in the bar.

Like it always had.

"I don't understand this," she said, stuttering a bit, unsure. Rattled.

"What don't you understand?"

"Why I— What this *thing* is with you."

"What thing would that be, exactly?"

"Why I feel…when we… I don't know you. I don't even think I like you much," she said, shaking her head. "But when I look at you, I…"

HBEXP79783

She remembered. Or some part of her did.

He took her chin between his forefinger and thumb.

Bo knew he should walk away, call a cab and leave. He should let this be.

But he wasn't going to.

"I think I know what you mean. I feel it, too," he said, his voice a whisper.

Her eyes widened, and without warning she turned her cheek into his palm. The light rub of her skin on his set his blood on fire, and sense evaporated. Everything was lost to the night, except being close to her, finally. Bo wanted to be closer.

He slid his hand back around her neck, bringing her forward until she bumped up against him. Then they were kissing, and it was the first time he could breathe in months.

He thought it would be a quick, gentle kiss, but it came on suddenly, like a summer storm. Her arms wrapped around him and she was pressing into him like she always had, as hungry as he was.

As he explored her throat before working his way up to her lips again, she pulled away, as if suddenly realizing what was happening. At the same time, voices rose in the parking lot behind them.

Bo could hardly think straight. He reached for her again.

"Erin, don't—"

She pushed past him, sprinting across the grass and out to the sidewalk.

He stared after her, some little thread of clarity returning.

What had he just done?

Pick up UNFORGETTABLE by Samantha Hunter, available December 17 wherever you buy Harlequin® Blaze® books.

The Wild Wild West

Ever since his father's famous bank robbery, rodeo cowboy Jesse James Chisholm has been the bad boy of Lost Gun, Texas. A rule breaker. A heartbreaker. But he's still haunted by his history, and the only girl who could match his wildness with her own—until she ditched her own bad-girl ways.

But mayor-elect Gracie Jones isn't quite the upstanding role model she projects. She may wear conservative skirts, but Jesse's return has stirred her long-slumbering wild side and a hunger for his rugged cowboy ways—talk about wild Wild West.

Pick up

Texas Outlaws: Jesse

by *Kimberly Raye,*

available January 2014 wherever you buy Harlequin Blaze books.

Your "Dating Boot Camp" Itinerary...

Day One

Fly to a luxurious resort in St. Bart's with your personalized
dating coach, Elisa Henderson. Show up on the plane with a guy
you just picked up. Find out Brett Jordan isn't just a drool-worthy
hottie—he's also a total player...and Elisa's former best friend!

Day Two

Be problematic. Disappear with a cute paparazzo.
Besides, Elisa and Brett are now alone in paradise, and Elisa's
about to break the first commandment of date coaching:
Thou Shall Not Sexily Ravage Your Client's Date. Lost clients,
naughty nighttime shenanigans, sleazy paparazzi...
Can Elisa avoid tarnishing her reputation?

Pick up

Still So Hot!

by *Serena Bell,*

available January 2014 wherever you buy
Harlequin Blaze books.

Red-Hot Reads
www.Harlequin.com

HB79785

HARLEQUIN®
A *Romance* FOR EVERY MOOD™

Stay up-to-date on all your
romance-reading news with the
Harlequin Shopping Guide,
featuring bestselling authors, exciting new
miniseries, books to watch and more!

The newest issue will be delivered right to you
with our compliments! There are 4 each year.

Signing up is easy.

EMAIL

ShoppingGuide@Harlequin.ca

WRITE TO US

HARLEQUIN BOOKS
Attention: Customer Service Department
P.O. Box 9057, Buffalo, NY 14269-9057

OR PHONE

1-800-873-8635 in the United States
1-888-343-9777 in Canada

Please allow 4-6 weeks for delivery of the first issue by mail.